THE CLOSER

THE CLOSER

AN ALL ABOUT THE DIAMOND ROMANCE

NAOMI SPRINGTHORP

The Closer
An All About the Diamond Romance (Book 5)
Copyright © 2019 Naomi Springthorp
Published by Naomi Springthorp
All rights reserved
Print Edition ISBN 978-1-949243-20-8

Cover Photographer: Tonya Clark - All About the Cover Photography
Cover Model: Matt Carothers
Graphic Designer: Irene Johnson johnsoni@mac.com
Editor: Katrina Fair

 Created with Vellum

*For my supportive friends. Team Naomi is strong.
Let's close this game!*

CHAPTER ONE

Houck

I t's been a shitty week and it's only Thursday. I've blown two saves and my girlfriend dumped me. She said I use her for sex and don't care about her. Neither are true, but I compare everyone to Angie and nobody comes close. I never should've let her walk away from me. I didn't know any better and she didn't want to traipse around the country following a minor league player. Why would she? We were friends and nothing more. We were college kids. She had her own goals and she achieved them without me. She never needed me, not the way I need her. They say the last person you think about when you go to bed and the first person you think about when you wake up is the one who's most important to you, it's always been Angie. Nights like this when I've blown the save, I wish I had her with me. The girlfriends come and go. I keep hoping there's one out there for me, I just haven't met her yet.

I swear Angie has a sixth sense. Most times I have her on my mind, she calls or something within a few days. Tonight a text comes in and it's not her typical fun message.

> Text from Angie - I need to see you
> Text from Angie - Already checked your schedule
> Text to Angie - You want to get together over the All-Star Break?
> Text from Angie - Just landed in San Diego

What the hell? I haven't been in the same room with her in thirteen years.

> Text to Angie - I'll be there to pick you up in twenty minutes or less
> Text from Angie - Thank you

I can't believe she's here. I don't have time to clean up, but I check the mirror to make sure I don't look like a fool. I shouldn't bother, she's a friend and has never been interested in me for anything more. But, when I remember her my blood pressure rises and I envision her with her head full of long fluffy dark blonde hair, wearing her cheerleading uniform with the short pleated skirt. Her legs toned, her breasts round, her strength and intelligence obvious. An unsolicited smile graces my face.

I slide into my car, voice texting her on the way to the airport, "On my way. Black Porsche 911."

Siri reads her reply to me, "Red dress."

I reply, "I know exactly what you look like," sending the message before I can reconsider and imagining her in a fitted red dress.

It's late and the airport is empty. I pull up to arrivals and she's standing in the beams of my headlights, gorgeous as always. I want to jump out and wrap my arms around her, kiss her senseless. I pull up calmly, hop out of my car and hug her, lifting her off her feet and kissing her cheek as I set her down. I load her suitcase into my backseat and chivalrously make sure she's in my car before I close her door for her. Everything about her is the same except the effect she has on me, which has become more potent. I attempt to calm myself down as I walk around to get in the driver's seat, but I'm consumed with how incredible she smells and how the kiss I gave her on the cheek should've been a closed mouth peck.

"I'm sorry about the short notice. I hope I'm not interfering with anything."

"You're always welcome. Is everything okay?" Wondering why she's here on such short notice, when she's always been prepared and calculated.

"I needed to see you," Her voice is different than I've ever heard. Her words pierce my heart with what I want her to mean, and I consider what the chances are that's her intent.

"Are you staying with me or do you have a hotel booked?" Please stay with me. Please say you're staying with me.

"I'd like to stay with you, if that's okay."

"Of course, you can use my guest room for as long as you want," unless you'd prefer to sleep in my bed, I will her to understand what I want and what she means to me.

"I don't have a plan, other than staying through the weekend and spending your off day with you. I'd like to watch you play. It's been years since I've been to a game."

I want to find out why she's here, but I'm happy to have her and don't want to push. She'll tell me when she's ready. "I'm the closer for the Seals. I don't get to pitch every game. I'm happy to get you a seat for the games this weekend."

She laughs, "I know you're the closer. I follow your career and your stats. I watch the highlights every time you pitch."

She watched me blow the last two saves. Is that why she's

3

here? She thinks I need help getting it together? "Look, I don't need a keeper. I'll bounce back from the blown saves. I'm perfectly fine by myself. The team's got my back. This isn't like back in college. I'm a confident grown man and I can take care of myself." I hear my words accompanied by my annoyed tone and wish I could suck them all back in before they reach her ears. I add quickly, "But, I'm happy to have you visit." I drive into the parking garage and park in my spot.

"I'm not here because you're off your game. You know how I feel about that, it's still just a game. No pitcher is perfect. Besides, when you need the baseball talk you always tell me you need it somehow and you haven't in years."

I shouldn't ask, "Then why are you here?" I offer her a hand out of my car and unload her suitcase.

"We're turning 35 this year. I'm not baby crazy, I'm not worried about my biological clock being a ticking time bomb. But, I do want things in my life and time is getting away from me. Every time a guy I'm dating starts to get serious, I dump him. Why are you still single?" Her big bright blue eyes search mine, waiting for an answer.

I've been waiting for you. Nobody compares to you. "I guess I haven't clicked with the right woman." Our conversation continues as we take the elevator up to my high-rise penthouse and I realize she's never been here. I hope she loves it, maybe she'll stay longer.

She nods her head, "What if we dumped the right one and we don't get another chance?"

"I didn't dump the right one. I found her. She never found me." Find me. Find me.

"You know who the one is?" She questions me and her voice gets higher pitched.

"Yes. I mean, I haven't tested the theory. I've never kissed her

4

or held her all night." I've wanted to since college. It's you, Angie. Tell me you want me, too.

Her voice is angry, "If there's a woman out there for you, why haven't you gone after her?"

"She lives far away and she's never been interested in me." The elevator opens and I lead her into my living room.

She stops in her tracks, not paying any attention to her surroundings, "Does she know how you feel?"

"She always seems to know everything."

"D, have you told her?" She shakes her head, "You're a major league baseball player and your record this year is 21 for 23, for Pete's sake!"

"My game has nothing to do with it, it can't be why she wants me. I've had too many of those and I've been dumped by the last one."

"Have you told her or not?"

"No."

"Wouldn't it be better if you were with her?"

"Yes. She's not interested."

"You can't be sure. You haven't told her."

"What if I tell her and she's not interested? Then I don't have her at all? I don't want to lose her completely."

"What are you losing out on by not telling her?"

She makes a good point. She probably wouldn't if she knew it was her. "Let me show you to your room," I refuse to respond to her question but bring her into the moment and she finally glances around.

"This is nice. Awesome view. I bet you spend a lot of time out on your balcony."

I smile, "Your room is on this side of the condo and you have your own bathroom. My master suite is on the other side of the condo, if you need me for anything." Fuck I'd love it if she needed me. "Please make yourself at home." I lay her suitcase on the bed and flip the light on in the bathroom. I open the closet door, showing her she has room to hang up her clothes.

"Thank you."

"I'll leave you to get unpacked and get some rest." I turn to walk away, but before I leave the room I continue with my back to her, "I'm happy to have you here with me. Stay as long as you want. Don't hesitate, if you need me."

I walk to my room and sit on the edge of my bed. I pick up the framed photo of us together from my nightstand, remembering the night it was taken. Her arms were wrapped around me and she was proud of me for pitching the complete game. I was a starter back then and I threw the complete game in 101 pitches. The experience wouldn't have been the same if she wasn't there with me. It was a milestone in my college baseball career and the part I remember in most detail is her. The excitement in her hands as she touched me. The natural curve of her lips as she squealed in celebration with me. Her fresh gaze on me, deep into my eyes. It was all going to change that night. I was sure she wanted to kiss me. I wished she wanted more from me, but it didn't happen. I should've known the game wouldn't have an affect on her, it never has. It's just a game.

CHAPTER TWO

Houck

I wake up early Friday morning and get up, quietly going about my morning routine. I don't want to disturb my houseguest. I wander into my kitchen after something to eat, wearing only my pajama pants and notice Angie's already up and enjoying my balcony. I change my plan and join her.

"Good morning, I hope you slept well." She's breathtaking standing there in the morning light with her hair blowing in the breeze. "Can I get you some breakfast? I need to go for a run, do you want to join me?" It's one of the things we used to do together in college.

"I'm up for a run. I love your view. It's a nice place you have here."

"Thanks," I get warm all over, and I catch her checking out my abs. "I have a few hours until I need to be at the stadium. Should be plenty of time to run and eat. There's a set of extra keys hanging on the refrigerator for you." We part to get ready and meet back in the living room ready to run.

I catch her staring at me again. There must be something different about me. It has been thirteen years. I hope it's not a bad thing. "What distance do you want to run?"

"I can always go for another run after you go to the stadium if we don't go far enough."

I glare at her and shake my head while we stretch, "I have stairs in my run. Let's go." We start off slow and pick up speed as we go. I lead and take her running through the East Village to the Harbor Drive Pedestrian Bridge. We run up the stairs and across the bridge, then down the other side. I watch in case she wants to stop and take in the view, but she seems to be more focused on me. Probably her competitive spirit making sure she keeps up with me. We run along the marina, then up and over the stairs at the convention center a few times before we take the paths at the marina parks. I lead her out the Embarcadero to Survivor's Park and back to run the Harbor path. "Too much?"

"It's a start," she winks at me and laughs.

We get home and she watches me in my kitchen, "What are you doing? I'm easy. Where's the cereal?"

I open the cabinet, "Which one would you like?" She points, choosing the healthy granola. I hand it to her with the milk. We sit and eat cereal together comfortably without words. I'm happy having her here, but my head keeps running possibilities. Is she right? Should I tell her she's the one? I wish she'd tell me why she's here.

Angie

This was a crazy idea. Why did I fly to San Diego? I've never done anything this spontaneous. I shouldn't ask why. I'm fully aware and I blame my business partner, Lucy. She's getting married and taking a class with her fiancé through their church. She's such a good girl. I could never take a class at the church. Honestly, I'm not sure I'm marriage material. She shared the lessons they did in the class and one of them hit me hard. If it was a rock, my windshield would be shattered into a zillion pieces. As it is, it sent my heart and brain into a tizzy. It's a workbook page with questions and you have to fill in the answers. Then you take the answers, only the answers, and create a list.

1. Who's presence makes you feel calm?
2. When you have something to celebrate, who do you want to tell?
3. Who's the first person you think of when you wake up in the morning?
4. Who do you enjoy spending time with?
5. Who has the same fitness and eating habits as you?
6. Who do you see when you think of the future?
7. Who's the last person you think of when you go to sleep?
8. Who do you dream about?
9. Who can't you live without?
10. Who makes you feel protected?

1. If you answered the same name to all of these questions with the name of your fiancé, congrats! You've found the right one.
2. If you answered multiple names and not only your fiancé, you might want to explore your options and make sure you're doing what's right for you.
3. If you answered the same name to all or most of these questions and you're not engaged, consider the following and don't waste time you could be spending with the one:

Does this person make you feel special?

Is this person always available for you and ready to do whatever they can for you?

Do you have a solid foundation of friendship?

What has stopped a relationship with this person from progressing in the past?

Have you ever been in a romantic relationship with this person? If no, it might be worth exploring.
Go kiss them already!

Anyway, point is, hell I don't need to explain to you. I'm sure you already get it. The answer to the first ten questions were the same—Super D. And, yes, it did occur to me that this pre-marital exercise feels a lot like a quiz from a fashion magazine. Regardless, it left me reflecting on the time I've spent with him and how much time I spend working and how the years keep flying by. I don't know if I want kids or not, it might depend on who the guy is. But, at this rate I'll never find out because I'll never pick the guy. Truth is, he's only a friend, though I've compared other men to him. Why shouldn't I consider him as a potential mate? Seriously, he checks off all the insignificant boxes, too. He has money, he won't be mooching off me and if he did, he'd be let down because I can't support his lifestyle with the penthouse he lives in. He's handsome and has a hot bod. I don't remember him having all those abs the last time I saw him. He should really think twice before he exposes a woman to his shirtless body. And those pajama pants? They left nothing to the imagination. I'm pretty sure he was going commando. He's a professional athlete. What more could I want?

I was going to spend today getting comfortable with the surroundings and kiss him tomorrow. But, who's this woman he's meant to be with? How have I never heard of this person before? Maybe he's wrong? He's a guy, he's most likely wrong part of the time. He doesn't think she's interested, that's in my favor. How'd he say it? 'He's never tested the theory.' I'd like him to kiss me and hold me all night. It would answer all of my questions.

"Did you hear me?" He asks.

"What?"

"I was talking to you."

"Sorry, not sure where my brain was," Lies, you have a fine ass.

He shakes his head, "I have to go to the stadium. I'll text you in a bit with your ticket information. You're welcome to use the jacuzzi tub in my bathroom. Eat whatever you want. Text me if you need anything. I'm texting you additional contact info in case it's an emergency, I don't always have my phone on me. Game starts at 7:05pm tonight."

Text from Super D - shared contact Carter
Text from Super D - Carter is the Clubhouse Manager. He can find me if you can't get me for some reason.

"See you tonight. Hope you enjoy the game." He turns to walk out and stops, "Hey, do you want to go out for a late dinner after the game tonight or maybe dessert?"

I smile, "Dessert sounds delicious."

He nods and steps onto the elevator.

Dessert could be interesting. He means ice cream or something, but my mind is going now.

CHAPTER THREE

Houck

I walk into the clubhouse and find Carter, "Hey, can you put my friend, Angie, on the early entry list? I need tickets for this weekend's games for her, too."

Seno walking by hears me talking to Carter, "Angie? Isn't she the one you told me about?"

"Yep." He high-fives me. "Nope, she's visiting for a few days. Showed up last night and she hasn't told me why. I'm not complaining."

Carter interjects, "Where do you want her to sit?"

"Best seat you've got."

Seno adds, "Put her next to Sherry, so she's not by herself."

"Works for me," Houck agrees. "Can you get her a jersey and cap, too?"

"Sure, with Houck on them?"

"Yeah, I guess."

"You don't want her to wear your name?" Seno questions me.

I chuckle, aware how this is going to sound, "She calls me

Super D." They both stare at me waiting for more. "She never thought Doug was a good enough name for me. Originally it was Super Doug, but you know how nicknames change."

"Super D it is. Any idea what size?"

"Misses jersey size medium. Can you charge anything she wants at the stadium to my account? I don't want her paying for anything. I want her to feel special. And, can you deliver everything to her at my place? She's not a fan of surprises."

Carter willingly goes along with it, "No problem. Easy enough since you live across the street."

"Thanks."

Text to Angie - Carter is going to deliver your tickets to you at my place. He has a key. He's a short bald man.
Text to Angie - Batting Practice is at 4pm. You're on the early entry list if you want to come watch.
Text from Angie - I'd love to!
Text from Angie - Going to try out your jacuzzi tub. I'll be at the stadium later.

And now I'm imagining her naked in my tub. I want to be naked in my tub with her.

Angie

When he said jacuzzi tub I pictured a tub with jets, not a jacuzzi fit for four grown adults. I could swim in this thing. I turn the water on, and let it start filling up while I get a change of clothes and grab a magazine from his coffee table. He's got music set up to pipe throughout his condo, I hit shuffle and go for luck. The sound of guitar strings and "Angela" by the Lumineers fills the room. I walk into his bathroom and strip naked, setting my phone and the magazine to the side while I climb into the tub. The jets blowing against me and the hot water are a perfect combination. Relaxing. I bet he uses the jacuzzi. We could both fit in the jacuzzi together with no problem. Maybe we can skinny dip in the jacuzzi together later. It would be better than dessert, or maybe it could be dessert. It would definitely melt the ice. Who am I kidding? That's not what I want. It is what I want, but not quick. For now, I'll soak here and daydream about the possibilities. Would he hold me in his lap and kiss me? Would he take control and splash water all over his bathroom while he takes me, claiming me as his? Maybe he's not a do it in the jacuzzi kind of guy. Maybe some warming up naked together, making out, hot heavy...

He walks in and finds me in his tub, jets on and water up to my neck. I'm relaxing and my eyes are closed. My hair tied up in a loose bun on top of my head. He pulls his shirt off, showing me his bare chest and abs. He turns around and drops his pants going commando, showing me his magnificent ass. He climbs in with me, sitting across from me with his feet stretched out at my sides. His hands out of sight under the water, reaching for me and caressing my leg. I go to him and his eyes search mine, finding what he wants his smile brightens and he pulls me down to him. Our lips meeting for the first time. Why didn't we kiss before? The heat between us is instantaneous, but we aren't ready for more. We pull back and smile at each other happily, both of us wanting each other for the first time. Holding each other is more than I ever dreamed would happen, but this is more. This is a need to be close to each other, explore each other, finally not worry if the other is interested and simply be together. His arm is holding me to him and his hand is at the back of my head. My arms are around his neck with one hand climbing up into his short brown hair and massaging his head. His other head is against my leg, but I'm not ready for him. I don't want to miss this new stage of us. We kiss sweetly, turning more heated with each passing second. He licks my lip and I open my mouth for him, kissing him deeply. Wanting more, but trying to hold back. He holds me close to him and keeps kissing me, not anything more. Simply holding my naked body against his and worshiping my lips. Why did I wait for this? Is he what I've been waiting for? He's been right here all along. He's all man and he's been waiting to be mine.

I hear a noise and I'm pulled from my daydream.

"Hello? It's Carter."

"Sorry, in the tub."

"No problem. I'm leaving tickets for all the games this weekend, a temporary access card so you can get in early, and a present from Houck on the kitchen island."

"Thank you."

"Enjoy your bath."

The elevator door closes and I listen to make sure he's gone. I get out of the tub and wrap a towel around my body, anxious to find what he left for me. I go to the kitchen and the first thing I see is a jersey with his number 18 and the name Super D. I get closer and find a matching cap. The jersey is even the right size. I open the envelope Carter left on the counter and find a note:

Angie,

Here are your tickets to this weekend's games. Use the card to get in early and to pay for anything you want while you're at the stadium. For early entry, use the VIP entrance near the home plate gate. Batting Practice is at 4pm. You can sit in your assigned seat for BP or anywhere you'd like on the field level, I suggest behind the Seals dugout.

Go Seals!
Carter

I'm standing in the kitchen, wearing only a towel when the door opens again. I've got to get used to this penthouse elevator. I consider running for it, but there's no time.

Houck

She's naked in my kitchen. She has a towel wrapped around her and it could fall off at any time. I've dreamt about having her in my kitchen in many different ways. She's always barefoot and naked, though I've never actually seen her naked. Her hair, piled on top of her head, leaves her neck and shoulders exposed. I'm staring at her and I can't take my eyes off her. I need to say something. Every second that passes makes me more of a creep. Then again, she's the one naked in my kitchen. "Hi, just want to check on you and make sure you have everything you need." How about me? Do you need me? I want you.

"I'm good." She steps from around the island and I can see the slit of the towel up to the top of her thigh. "Thanks for the jersey."

"You look good," I can't take my eyes off of her. She's better than good, she's stunning. "You're welcome." I fidget nervously. I want to reach for her and hold her, but I need to get back to the stadium. We're not that kind of friends. We've always been friends, nothing more. I've always wanted it to be more. Why didn't I kiss her thirteen years ago?

"Thanks," I swear she blushes.

I turn away quickly, "I have to get back. See you at the stadium." The elevator door couldn't close quick enough. I need to get out of here before I do something I shouldn't.

Angie

I get ready for the game, putting a low-cut snug-fitting tank on under my jersey. I button the lower buttons on the jersey and leave the top open. It's cute with my matching bikini panties and

I consider taking a pic for future use, or maybe to send to D now. Too much for an ice-breaker? Probably. He was surprised and uncomfortable seeing me in a towel. I slide into my skinny jeans and put my sneakers on. I let my hair down and brush it out, trying the cap to figure out how I want to wear it. I leave my hair down and put the cap over it.

I'm anxious to see BP. He probably won't hit. Why would he? He's the closer. Still, it's nice for him to get me in early. I toss the envelope Carter left for me and the extra keys to D's place in my bag and walk over to the stadium. The stadium is easy. Everyone treats me like I'm a queen when I flash the card Carter gave me. The stadium is empty, except for workers prepping food and cleaning. There are only a few people in the stands and some men in team polos on the concourse. A couple players are on the field throwing the ball. There's one woman sitting behind the Seals dugout, and not another single butt in a seat. I follow her lead and sit a few seats away from her. She's focused on one player, I'm guessing it's her husband because she's noticeably pregnant.

"Hi, you must be Angie," a short bald man startles me. "I'm Carter."

"Nice to meet you. Thanks for setting this up for me."

"This is all Houck. I wanted to introduce you to Sherry, since your seat is near hers all weekend and she knows the drill on everything."

The pregnant woman turns briefly, "Hi, nice to meet you." Then back to watching BP, obviously taking it seriously. "Looking good, Seno!" She calls out. One of the players grins at her happily.

"I'll leave you two to get to know each other. Let me know if you need anything," Carter excuses himself.

It's refreshing to see two people who are meant for each other, have found each other. Their connection is clear, even with the distance between them. My heart warms at the thought and my mind wanders, are D and I meant to be together?

"There's your guy," Sherry points to Houck as he walks out onto the field.

"He's not my guy. We're friends," and I wonder why I point it out when I wish he was my guy. Or, maybe, want to find out if he's supposed to be my guy.

She turns and focuses on me, taking her eyes off the field. "Sorry, I shouldn't have assumed."

"It's okay. I've wondered what it would be like if he was."

"What's stopping you?"

"I don't want to mess up our friendship, but I'm here to find out if it's worth the friendship risk and if there are any signs he's interested."

"Does he know?"

"He doesn't know why I'm here. I hopped a flight to San Diego and called him when I landed."

Sherry yells at the field, "Seno!" and waves him over.

He comes up to the stands and puts his arms around her after his next turn at bat, "Is everything okay, my queen?"

She smiles like her world is complete, "I'm fine, wanted you to meet Houck's friend. This is Angie."

He shakes my hand, "Nice to finally meet you. I've heard a lot about you."

"Why would you hear about me?" I laugh.

His eyes widen, "It was all positive. I have to get back." He kisses Sherry on the cheek and runs back to the field quickly, not wanting to elaborate.

Sherry turns back to watch BP, "There's your sign. These guys don't talk about 'friends' enough for their teammates to know who they are."

Seno yells to the outfield, but I can't understand what he says. He points at me. D shakes him off. He yells again, loud and clear this time, "Never shake off your catcher. I call the game." D shakes his head, irritated and runs toward Seno. I watch their conversation, but can't make out the details. Seno hands D a bat and puts a helmet on his head with a big grin on his face. D complains and curses him out. "Shut up and trust me. Hit the fucking ball!" Carter's behind home plate chuckling and a couple of the other players are chiming in on the situation. D walks up to bat awkwardly and uncomfortable with a bat in his hands. Banter around the backstop continues, a combination of jibes and encouragement.

The first ball, he swings and hits the ball up the third base line. I call out, "Wooo wooo, go D!"

His stance changes, he's more comfortable. The second ball, and he swings like he means it, but misses the ball completely. I hear him cursing from my seat. The third ball, and he smacks it out of the park. I stand up and cheer, "Yeah! Go Super D!"

"Isn't it fun to cheer when your guy does something?" Sherry grins. "He may not be your guy yet, but he's your guy."

Fourth ball and he hits another home run. I cheer for him again and get more enthusiastic, remembering my cheerleading days. I know how to turn on the pep and root for my guy. My guy? We'll revisit that later. Fifth ball and he hits it to the outfield wall, disturbing the guys standing out there doing nothing. His turn is over and he goes back to Seno who points at me. D shakes his head and gazes up at me in the stands. His smile is brighter the longer he's focused on me. He runs up to my seat, "The team is picking on me because I have a hot blonde visitor and I hadn't come up to say hi yet."

"Maybe you should hook me up." I say laughing and his expression changes I test the water further, "Which one said I'm a hot blonde?"

He leans in to my ear and whispers, "Me." He kisses my cheek the same way he did last night when he picked me up at the airport, more than a peck on the cheek and runs back to the field.

Me? He considers me a hot blonde? Did I hear him correctly? "Is there a player on the team with a name that sounds like 'me'?" I ask Sherry.

She rolls her eyes at me, "I told you he's your guy."

"What if he's not? What if I test the theory and it all goes to shit? What if it ends our friendship?"

"What do you mean? Test the theory? This is love, nothing scientific about it."

Love? I hadn't even considered love. I guess its part of being the one. You know, those stupid pre-marital classes should be more specific about things. "D said he knows who the one for him is, but she isn't interested. He said he hasn't kissed her or held her all night, he hasn't tested the theory." My brain is still stuck on 'love' while I rattle off the words. "You look happy with your man. You love him?"

Sherry giggles, "I am and very much. I didn't know this connection was possible until I met Rick. I wouldn't trade it for anything."

"I've never done the love thing."

"You don't choose love. It finds you. When it finds you, you don't have a choice."

BP is over and Seno runs up in time to hear Sherry say those words. "And, I'm glad it did." He lifts her off her feet and kisses her. He leans his forehead to hers without putting her down, "How's Baby Seno treating you today?"

"Baby cheers when I cheer and I approve of the behavior," her happiness is overflowing.

He hugs her and sets her on her feet. They both palm her belly and make eye contact. "I love you, my queen. Don't over do it. I'll meet you at the car after the game."

"Make it a win!" She tells him and he takes off for the dug out.

Their interaction gives me hope. "Are you for real? Your whole demeanor changes and you smile bigger in his presence."

"What do you think you did when Houck was here to say hi?"

I gasp internally. "There's no way."

"You did. He did, too."

"Are you telling me to test the theory?"

"Finally, you're catching on. Have you considered you might be the one who isn't interested in? Then again, what if you're not. Maybe he needs to know you're an option." She stops, "Now, I need to watch BP for the other team and report in. We're winning this season and it's one of the ways I contribute."

I sit quietly and watch the rest of BP. Honestly, I can't tell you a thing about BP. My head is reeling at the thought of being with D. Taking a chance. The possibility of love. What's the first step? Luckily I have the whole baseball game to figure it out. 48 outs and hopefully he'll come in to close. I'd love to watch him pitch and get the save.

Houck

Why did I tell her she's a hot blonde? Whispering in her ear and kissing her inappropriately on the cheek again? Having her here makes it hard to control myself. The text messages and phone calls at all hours are one thing. It doesn't matter if I had a girlfriend or not, I've always been able to be there for her whenever she wanted me. I always found a way to get away for Angie. A phone call from Angie was more important than anything with any other girl. That's bad, but it's true. I guess they've all been placeholders. Maybe the last one was right, maybe I didn't care. Maybe I didn't care about any of them. Having Angie here makes them all seem insignificant. Shit. I never got any of them in for early BP. I'd get them a ticket to the game if they asked, but never anywhere special. With Angie, everything needs to be the best and I want her to have everything she wants.

Seno and Carter walk up to me, Carter starts, "Anything else I can help you with for Angie?"

"Yeah, can you take her my hoodie? I don't want her to get cold tonight."

"I already made her one up with Super D and your number on it," he grins like a know-it-all. "I'll take it to her before the game starts. She has food service at her seat and the server has already been notified she's to charge your account."

"Thanks." I want to talk to her, but Seno is standing in front of me.

"I already talked to Skip and told him we need you to come in to close tonight. I'm not giving up any runs to get you a save, but most likely you'll be pitching the 9th. She needs to watch you pitch and win. Women like winners." He has it all planned out. "I know you've had a couple bad outings. Nobody's perfect. There's nobody I'd rather have closing for my team. It's probably the only two blown saves you'll have all season. I'm happy you got them out of the way early." He smiles deviously, "Now, tell me you want this woman and the texts I got from Sherry aren't crazy."

"What?"

"She's been talking to Sherry. Never mind. See you on the field," he high-fives me and walks away.

I wonder what they've been talking about.

24

Text to Angie - Did you enjoy BP?
Text to Angie - You have food service at your seat tonight. It's
already set up. You don't need money.
Text to Angie - Carter's bringing you a hoodie for me.

She isn't answering. I start to get ready for the game and my
phone lights up.

Text from Angie - BP was fun
Text from Angie - You didn't have to do all this for me
Text from Angie - Thank you (picture of Angie in her Seals
jersey and cap)
Text from Angie - Ordered a hot dog and beer. Saving room
for dessert.

Fuck, she's hot in my jersey.

CHAPTER FOUR

Angie

Text from D - I'll meet you at my place after the game.

Text to D - What's for dessert?

Text from D - Whatever you want.

I want you. Can I have you? Maybe I need to test his theory. We need to kiss and he needs to hold me all night. How do I make both of those things happen?

Text to D - Where's your favorite place to have dessert?

Text from D - My bed, with a big bowl of ice cream or gelato watching a movie.

Ding! Ding! Ding! We have a winner!

Text to D - Sounds like a plan.

Text from D - You're going to sit in my bed with me and eat ice cream?

Text to D - Yea, is that a problem?

Text from D - No. You pick the movie.

Text to D - How have I never heard about the girl who's the one for you?

Text from D - Time for the game. We'll talk later.

Text to D - Have a good game.

I'm going to sit in bed with him and watch a movie with a bowl of ice cream.

I sit with Sherry and watch the team warm up. The relief pitchers walk out to the bullpen in a group before the game starts. D is leading the bunch. It's fun to cheer with Sherry and get involved in the game. I haven't had the opportunity to enjoy a baseball game like this since college.

I remember the night D pitched the complete game. It's probably the only time I ever considered kissing him, until recently. If my business partner wasn't getting married, I'd probably still be in control of my world and not wondering if I'm missing out. Have I been missing out on D all this time?

It's the bottom of the 8th inning and the Seals are ahead by 3. The score is 4-1 Seals. They flash the bullpen up on the big screen and D is warming up. D is warming up! He's damn fine in his uniform. I don't remember him being so much of a man. I guess it was college. He probably hadn't filled out yet and he definitely hadn't had the opportunity to work out with a professional baseball team. There's no denying it, he's hot. He's tall with larger than average shoulders. His hair is cut short and clean. His pants are snug around his ass and he's wearing them long, down to his cleats. No stirrups or fun socks, he's all business.

End of the 8th inning and no score change. The stadium goes

dark and the speakers start blaring "Sex Type Thing" by Stone Temple Pilots. The light bars are blue with a neon green line showing the beat of the music, then flashing to Houck. The big screen changes back and forth from the ball in his hand to his eyes staring you down. His gorgeous grey eyes staring straight into my heart. It's hot, or maybe it's me. He can stare at me like that any time he wants. I find myself standing up and cheering for him as he runs to the mound. "Let's do this, Super D! Wooooo!" Did he smile at me? It's probably in my head. Seno's behind home plate and ready to go. D throws him a few pitches and the first hitter of the 9th inning steps into the batter's box. First pitch and he's challenging the hitter with a 100 mile per hour fastball right up the pipe. The bat connects and it's a come backer, straight at D and he catches it. "Wooooooooooooo!" One out. Second hitter and he throws him a fastball low on the outside corner, he gets the strike call. Second pitch, exactly the same spot and the hitter reaches for it smacking it down the first base line. First baseman, Kris Martin, grabs it and tags the runner out. "Yes! Go D! Wooo!" I'm dancing around and all the Seals fans are on their feet for the last out of the game. First pitch, he throws a curve for a strike. Second pitch, 98 mile per hour fastball on the outside corner for a called strike. Count is 0-2. Third pitch, 102 mile per hour fastball but it's off the plate. Fourth pitch, heater straight down the middle, batter swings and misses. Strike out, the Seals win and D gets the save. I scream out at the top of my lungs, "Woooooo! Go Super D!" and I dance around happy.

He's staring at me and smiling. He meets Seno halfway between the mound and home plate for a bro hug. They high-five the rest of the team in celebration of the win and the on field reporter grabs him for an interview. They show it up on the big screen.

"Doug, your fastball tonight was on point. You were clocked

at up to 102 miles per hour, your fastest pitch of the season so far. Have you been working on pitch speed?"

"I had a lot of adrenaline going into the game tonight. It felt good to get it out there. I've been throwing 100 miles per hour routinely in practices."

"How do you feel getting the save tonight after blowing the save on both of the last two outings?"

"I never want to let me team down, but nobody's perfect. I wanted to get it done in three tonight and show them I'm the closer. I think I achieved that."

"You most certainly did and brought some amazing heat. Great job."

"Thanks."

***

Houck

I search for Angie in her seat or around the dug out after my interview, but she's not there. It's okay, she'll be at my place waiting for me.

My mind switches gears. She's going to be in my bed with me eating ice cream? How's this going to work? I need to make sure I stay in control. Fuck, I've dreamt about having her in my bed and it's always amazing, but definitely not in control. In my dreams, I hold her close to me and kiss her until she gives herself to me. She gives up control to me completely. There's no words saying it, her actions are all it takes. She's mine before I do anything more than kiss her. Fuck, kissing her. Kissing her is a drug I can't get enough of, better than the adrenaline rush I get on the mound when I get the save. I have to kiss her. I need to taste her. It's a dream, not reality. I dream about her, aware it'll never happen and with no consideration for it even being a possibility. Is there a chance it could be real? No, she's not interested. Don't get your hopes up. Stay in control. Enjoy the time while you have her here. No more whispering things in her ear. No more kissing her on the cheek. She's going to be in my bed. My mind races because I know what happens when a woman is in my bed. This isn't some hook up. This is Angie. I take a deep breath to center myself. The bed is a big sofa. We'll prop the pillows up against my headboard to lean against and sit on top of the bedspread. Right. I can do this. What if we fall asleep? Doesn't matter, we'll be sleeping. I'm sure she'll get up and go to her room when she wakes up in the middle of the night. It's fine.

"Hey!" Seno calls out to me, pulling me out of my head, "You okay?"

"Yeah."

"You look confused. What's up?"

"Nothing." He motions for me to tell him and I spill, "Angie's going to watch a movie with me in my bed tonight."

"What's the problem?"

"She's not interested and I want more. It's always been this way."

"Why's she here? What if she's interested?"

"I'd love it, but..." he interrupts me.

"I'm just saying, maybe you shouldn't rule it out."

"I'm open to the possibility. She's more beautiful now than I remember her being before. The part that gets me though, is how she's still her. You know? She hasn't changed. I talk to her all the time, but it's different when she's actually here. The time apart doesn't matter. It's like we've spent everyday since college together." I stop and close my eyes, "That's the problem. I don't want to lose her. What if I do the wrong thing and she's gone forever?"

"What if you don't do anything and you never find out? What are you missing out on by not trying for more with her?" He turns to walk out of the clubhouse, "Good luck."

I'm going to enjoy spending the evening with her. Maybe tomorrow I can try something new.

> Text to Angie - I have vanilla and chocolate chip ice cream in my freezer.
> Text to Angie - Does that work or would you prefer to go get ice cream and take it back to my place?
> Text from Angie - Works for me. I'll be here when you get home.

I'm warm all over, she's at my place waiting for me. I get out of the clubhouse in half the time I normally take and don't hang out with the team.

———

Angie

I change into my soft cotton PJ shorts and the faded Seals T-shirt I've had since D was signed by the Seals, comfy and ready to watch a movie. I skim through his movie collection and choose a romantic comedy. There's only a couple and they both feature baseball. I go with Bull Durham because I love the speeches and the passion in the sexy scenes.

I walk to his bedroom and lean in the doorway studying his bed. The leather upholstered headboard has aged-brass fasteners and beading. The king sized bed is covered with an oversized warm dark chocolate comforter, accented with a bordeaux throw and pillows. The materials and colors are masculine, yet soft and luxurious. It's inviting to me. His room is large with a full wall of windows covered in blackout draperies to match his comforter. The walls are all off-white and he has some enlarged photos from his college team on the wall, along with a framed print of a baseball diagram. A framed photo on his nightstand gets my attention and I go to it, imagining it's a picture of his family who I haven't seen in years. But, it's not. It's us in college and my arm's around him, gazing up at him as if he's the only one who matters. He's smiling back at me with heavy hooded eyes. He wanted me then.

What am I doing here?

The elevator opens, and he calls out, "I'm home. Angie?"

"I'm in here," I respond without thinking. Why am I in his room? "Checking if I should bring my pillow and blanket with me to watch the movie."

I turn to find him standing in the doorway, "You won't need them."

Text from Lucy - Do you want to learn about today's lesson?
Text to Lucy - I'm still stuck on the last lesson. Thank you very much.
Text from Lucy - Did you find out yet?
Text to Lucy - Working up to it.
Text from Lucy - Stop wasting time. I need you working, not distracted by a man.

"Are you okay?" D asks.

"Perfectly fine. Business partner getting me caught up on today. It won't take long." I sit down on the edge of his bed while I text.

Text from Lucy - You're smart and gorgeous. Any man who doesn't want you is an idiot.

Text from Lucy - Your friends aren't idiots. Stop waiting. Do it.

Text from Lucy - Today's lesson was about being confident and comfortable in your relationship.

Text to Lucy - Stop! I'm not ready for the next lesson.

Text from Lucy - I think you're already comfortable, show your confidence.

Text to Lucy - How was business today?

Text from Lucy - Everything is under control. Handle your business.

There's a reason we're successful business partners. We support each other and push each other when we need to. I need to listen to her. Shit. Sherry said the same thing.

D walks back into his room with a huge bowl of ice cream, "I went with chocolate chip. Is it still your go-to flavor?"

"Yes, thank you," I say as he hands me the bowl with two spoons and disappears into his closet.

He comes back wearing sweatpants and a threadbare concert T-shirt. Damn he's sexy. I'm surprised the T-shirt is staying together as it's stretched across his chest and shoulders. Ugh, and he smells all fresh and manly. "Great game tonight. You were perfect on the mound. Form, speed, location, everything on point. I guess you don't need me to tell you, the on-field reporter already did."

"It means more from you. You're never here. I'm glad you got to see me pitch." He smiles at me and stretches out on his bed, leaning back against the headboard. He takes the bowl of ice cream from me and I pull my feet up onto his bed as I move to sit next to him, so we can share.

He starts the movie with a remote without getting up. It's nice he's still the same guy. Yes, he lives in a penthouse and has some high-end things, but he's still him. He's still happy to stay home and hang out in an old T-shirt and sweats with a bowl of ice cream. Nothing snooty like Kulfi or Lavender Honey, simply the old standard vanilla or chocolate chip. He's relaxed and comfortable with himself the way he is. It makes him even sexier.

I take a spoon and dig into the bowl for a bite of ice cream, moving in closer and leaning against him in the process. He's warm and I don't understand how the ice cream in his hands hasn't melted. I take another bite and rub against him, waiting for a reaction and not getting one.

"So, tell me about the woman who's the one and isn't interested. Why haven't you told me about her?"

He chuckles, "She's successful and doesn't need a man in her life. Men are complications for her."

"She may not need a man, but it doesn't mean she doesn't want one. I'm guessing it's a possibility."

"Maybe, but she's never shown any signs of interest in me and she's had boyfriends right in front of me."

"How long have you known her?"

"Since college."

"Have I met her?"

"We don't need to have this conversation. It's not going to make a difference. It's not going to suddenly make her interested in me," his frustration shows.

I back off on the conversation. I consider who it could be and how I could've missed it back then. We were together all the time. My boyfriends used to get irritated at how much time I spent with D. Wait. Could he be talking about me? I go for another bite of ice cream and make myself comfortable up against him. He doesn't move or change positions, he let's me do what I want and shifts to suit me. He sets the empty bowl on his nightstand and comes back to exactly where he was, trying not to disturb my position. I lean my head on his shoulder and he rests his arm around my shoulders. Not holding me to him, simply getting more comfortable. Either way, it's nice to have his arm around me. We watch the movie together and my head runs away imagining how D could be the one. I'm comfortable with him and he's sexy and we get along, we've always gotten along. Is the girl who's not interested me? I need to show him a sign. He needs to know maybe I'm interested. Damn it! I'm interested.

I reach for the throw to cover my legs and he puts his legs over mine to help warm me up. I snuggle into him and he holds me there, like it's where I belong.

CHAPTER FIVE

Houck

Is this Angie? In my bed, up against me with my arm around her?

"D?"

"Yeah?"

"You think I'm a hot blonde?"

"Always have, Ang." I glance at her face to catch her smiling, but she's sleeping. I pull her in closer to me with both arms around her. "Do you want to stay here with me tonight?" I ask softly.

She mumbles something I can't determine, but her reaction is positive.

I hold her with one arm and adjust the pillows, sliding us down to lie on the mattress. She cuddles into me, nuzzling into my chest and my heart beats harder. I hold her, content. The theory is getting tested voluntarily. I'm holding her all night tonight and it just happened, I didn't have to do anything to get here. I consider step two of the test. Will the kiss come to me on it's own, too?

I'm holding her and her body is next to mine. She's wrapped her arm around me. I can't believe I've never held her before.

Houck

I wake up in the middle of the night and it's my dream. I'm holding her in my arms and she's wrapped around me. I didn't believe this would ever happen. I've wanted her for so long. I kiss her forehead and glide my foot along her bare legs, she's cold. I pull the blankets back carefully, trying not to wake her. I whisper to her, "Angie, you're cold. I'm getting us under the blankets and making sure you get warm. Sleep, everything is fine. D is taking care of you." I pull the blankets down behind me. I move back on the bed and take her with me, then pull the blankets up over us.

"Thank you, D," she sighs sweetly without opening her eyes.

Her sweet tone tears at my heart and I hold her tight, "I'll always take care of you."

Houck

I wake up again and she's gone. I didn't get to hold her all night. She must not have wanted to be in my bed. What was I thinking? Of course she doesn't want to be with me. She's not interested in me. She fell asleep. I take my shirt off and shed my sweatpants. I'm ready to go back to sleep when the toilet flushes and Angie walks out of my master bathroom. I'm stripped to my boxer briefs. Is she coming back to my bed or what? Come back to bed, Angie. Please, come back to bed. She walks straight back to my bed and climbs under the blankets, reaching for me and snuggling against me. She didn't fully wake up, but she's aware something is different. Her hands roam my body from my waist across my abs to my chest. She buries her cold feet between my legs. She giggles happily and is back to sleep with her fingers splayed across my chest within seconds. Fuck! Her hand touching my bare chest lights me on fire. She makes me want more. I'd give her anything, everything, if she'd stay with me.

Angie

I wake up in bed with D. His arms are wrapped around me and holding me close to him. I'm nuzzled against him with my hand on his bare chest and my feet snuggled between his legs. What happened? How did I get here? When did he lose his shirt? And pants? Should I get out of bed and go to my own room? My lips are pressed to his chest and he kisses my forehead. He's awake. "I'm sorry. I didn't mean to invade your bed." I'm surprised at myself and unsure about the situation. I move to get out of bed, but he stops me.

His grip on me tightens. "Please stay here with me," he says in a heartfelt raspy tone.

"Okay." My whole body relaxes. He wants me here. "D?"

"Yeah?"

"What are we doing?"

"Sleeping."

"You know what I mean."

"Do you like my arms around you, holding you?" he asks me.

"Yes." It's what I want.

"Then enjoy it with me. We don't have to talk about it. I'll never do anything you don't want me to do."

"D, am I the one who's not interested?"

"Testing a theory."

That's not an answer. I kiss and explore his bare chest as I go back to sleep.

CHAPTER SIX

Angie

Waking up in his arms with my hands on his shirtless body may be the best thing I've ever experienced. He's a professional athlete and has the body to prove it. His thick, corded arms protect me while his hands are splayed across my back with need. His long muscular legs warm my always cold feet between his calves. His lips touch my forehead with his nose buried in my hair. More than any of the rest of it, it's D. My Super D I've talked to or text messaged almost everyday since college. He's always been there for me.

I lie quiet and still, wanting as much of him as I can get and appreciating his manly scent while I wait for him to wake up. I'm happy to stay right here all day, but he can't. I'll be going to the baseball game tonight to watch his team play and hopefully cheer for him pitching for the save again.

Houck

I don't want to move. I want everything to stay exactly the way it is right now. I've stayed in bed longer today than I ever do during the baseball season. This could be the only time I have Angie in my bed. Test the theory is a fine plan, but what did I learn? She appreciates my shirtless body. Does it mean she wants me? I need more. I need the kiss.

I kiss her forehead, "Ang? Are you awake?"

"Yeah. Good morning," she says softly and doesn't move

"Were you comfortable last night?"

"It was perfect. D, were you testing the theory?"

Angie

He pulls me against him, "I think the theory tested us." He gazes into my eyes and I can't help but to search his, wondering what his test results are and if they match the possessiveness he has in his hands. "Spend the night with me tonight?" He says low and raspy.

I smile and kiss his cheek while I glide my hand across his abs.

"I'm taking that as a yes."

"It's most definitely a yes." I stop and worry about what happens next. What about our friendship? "Are we still friends?"

"We'll always be friends. Nothing can change that."

What about part two of testing the theory? Will it happen? I don't want him questioning my intent, "I don't know who the one is that's not interested." I stop and drag my teeth across his earlobe, then whisper, "If it's me, you're wrong. I'm interested."

He pulls back away from me, holding me at arms length

while he reads my expression and body language. His eyes shine and he laughs, "The first time I kiss you can't be in my bed when I'm mostly naked."

"Why not?" I need to kiss him. I need answers. Everything's right and I don't want to wait anymore. I run my fingers through his hair and pull his lips to mine. Chaste, not pushing it further. I pull away and get out of his bed with him watching my every move.

"Ang?" He calls out to me as I'm about to leave his room. I turn to find him sitting up in bed with the blanket covering him up to his waist and his strong chest bare. His eyes catch mine and he grins, "Have dinner with me tonight after the game?"

"I'll be here. Good luck at the game today." I walk away, leaving him to get ready for work. I take a quick shower and throw on shorts and a tank top. I pour myself some juice and sit out on his balcony, enjoying the cool breeze and bright blue San Diego sky. I'm buzzing at the idea of being with D. Kissing him wasn't weird at all. In fact, I want more.

Houck

I lie back down and stretch out across my bed. She kissed me and walked away. She's spending the night with me tonight and we're having dinner together. I need to get ready and go to the stadium. Fuck! I need to kiss her. No time for distractions, I already stayed in bed too long. I clean up and get ready for work. I sit at my kitchen island and eat a bowl of cereal, noticing she's doing yoga in the sunlight on my balcony. Stretching and bending, slow and methodically. I can't help myself. She's sexy and I'm not leaving her wondering until after the game. I need more now.

I join her on my balcony. Her eyes are closed and her hands

are reaching for the sky. She's beautiful, calm and centered. I hesitate, examining every inch of her and suddenly worry the kiss might go bad. What if it's not special for her? Not the connection I'm anticipating? I don't have time for a second chance. It doesn't matter. I reach for her, leaning down to her ear I whisper, 'Angie." I kiss her in front of her ear and she gazes up at me. My arm is around her and my other hand in her hair, I press my lips to hers asking for more. Asking for everything she's willing to give me. She's the one, she's always been the one. Her soft lips receive me willingly and kiss me back. Our kiss turns open-mouthed, our lips meeting repeatedly. She wraps her arms around my neck and arches into me. My heart pounds. She wants me. I slide my tongue against her lips and she opens for me immediately, greeting my tongue with hers and I'm done. I tighten my grip on her and control the kiss, my body ready to explode. I taste every bit of her lips and our tongues dance together. Her hands pushing up into my hair like she's trying to hold on. I glide my hands down her body and lift her up against me. She clings to me, wrapping her legs around my waist and arms around my neck She throws her head back and giggles, then gazes straight into my eyes. "What are you looking for?" I ask her.

"I'm not sure."

"You don't need to look anymore. You found me."

"I have competition. Who's the one?" Her voice is concerned but confident.

I lean my forehead to hers and kiss her nose, "There's no competition. I didn't think you were interested in me."

She claims my mouth with hers leaving no question in my mind. She's more confident and forward than any woman I've been with. Not one of the skanks who goes straight for my dick because it's all they want. Is it because it's us or is she always aggressive? I'm hot all over, simply holding her and kissing her. This can't be like other women. I can't screw this up. She's only here a few days and this has to be at her pace. I can't carry her off to my room and fuck her, she's more than all of them together. This heat, her hands on me make my blood sizzle with desire. I've never wanted a woman more. I want her everywhere, not just wrapped around my cock. I tug on her sweet lips and I'm out of breath. I break the kiss and hug her close, whispering in her ear, "I'm all in. We don't need to rush us. Everything at your pace, Ang." I take a deep breath, "I need to get to the stadium, so I can pitch tonight. I'll be watching for you."

"I'll be there," she says as she slides down my body rubbing against my hard-on. "That's pleasing," she giggles. "We'll figure it out," she continues as she bites her lower lip.

I roll my eyes and give her a quick kiss before I run to the stadium. I'm glad I'm only across the street, I'd be late for sure. I adjust myself in the elevator and regain control.

I run into the stadium and Carter yells for me when I pass his office, "Houck!"

I turn around and lean in his doorway, "Yeah?"

"Running late?" he smiles. "Need assistance with anything today? BP is at 2:00."

"Can you arrange a candlelight dinner for two? After tonight's game?"

"Absolutely, where at?"

"My place on the balcony."

"No problem."

Text to Angie - BP at 2:00, game at 5:00 today
Text to Angie - Not that I'll be hitting
Text from Angie - I'll be there :)

Angie

There's a smile on my face I can't control. A man has never affected me this way. He's a tropical storm. Hot and sending lightning from my fingertips to my toes, leaving the thunder to rumble nervously in my belly. He's known I'm the one and didn't think I'm interested. Honestly, I hadn't considered him until Lucy and her pre-marital course. He's always been my friend D. That's it. Lying next to him last night, sleeping in his bed and simply being live, in person with him is a whole other ball game. I had to kiss him. I couldn't resist caressing his bare skin. He's known I'm the one all this time, and I didn't? Aren't women supposed to be more intuitive of these things? I guess I've always been more of a guy in some ways. I don't want to be a guy with D. Huh, what I found sliding down his body, Super D might be a description of him.

Since the game is earlier today, I don't have much time to get ready. I put my jersey and cap on over my shorts and tank top. I get distracted as I wander through his place and find myself leaning in the doorway to his bedroom. What am I doing here? I don't live here. I'm leaving in a few days. Can this work? Did I destroy our friendship? No. I can figure this out. But, right now all I can do is focus on his bed and the memory of his protective arms around me. The room is filled with his clean masculine scent and when I close my eyes he's pressing his lips to mine. I'm consumed by his heat and possessive fingers in my hair. Simply imagining him my pulse races and I'm unsure how I'm going to handle being near him alone tonight.

CHAPTER SEVEN

Angie

I find Sherry behind the dug out for batting practice and sit next to her. How does she do this everyday in her condition? Business alone could make it a challenge for me, but I'm not allowing any extra complications right now. I'm focusing on now and not how life will want to get in the way. "Hi, did I miss anything?"

"You're right on time," she turns and examines me, getting a big grin on her face. "Looks like you tested the theory with positive results."

I nod, "We'll find out after the game." We only kissed once, but damn was it an amazing kiss.

The team emerges from the dugout a few at a time. A bunch of pitchers walk to the outfield in a cluster and Seno drags D with him to take a turn at bat. Sherry yells at Seno and I follow suit loudly, "Go Super D!" She pats my knee and gives me a thumbs up. He smiles as he runs up to visit me. He grabs my hand and pulls me up out of my seat, then gazing into my eyes he kisses me.

Not a sweet peck, no this was more. His hands are on my face holding me where he wants me while he brushes his lips against mine, sucking and nibbling on them until my breath turns ragged.

He breaks the kiss to whisper, warm in my ear, "I want to kiss you all night long. I have fifteen years of imagining what it's like to kiss you to make up for. I'll be happy kissing you and holding you again tonight." His tone, sincere and raspy, hits me directly in the gut causing the thunder to rumble. He kisses me below my ear and lifts me up to kiss and nuzzle at my neck, driving me crazy. I whimper uncontrollably and wrap my legs around him right there in front of everyone. The team catcalls at us, woots, whistles, "Get it!" and "Houck's got a hottie."

I lean down to whisper in his ear, hard to speak because he has me worked up, "You make me hot. You make me want more than kissing. You make me lose control." I tug on his ear with my teeth and sigh, "I want you."

He whispers back to me, "I want you, too. We'll talk over dinner, this can't be a game. You're the only woman I want." He smiles at me and I nod at him in agreement. He gives me a quick peck on the lips as he sets me back on the ground and he's gone.

"Looks mind blowing to me," Sherry comments. "I remember those first kisses when he left me punch drunk. I thought I was crazy. It was the new guy excitement." She laughs, "It still happens."

I smile and focus on batting practice, or at least pretend to because I can't focus on anything except D and putting words together is a challenge. He's right, we can't be a game and we should do the adult thing and talk about it, but it's new and I want to enjoy it. It's wrong, but I'd take his D out for a ride and find out if it should be the Super D. Not in a bad way, it's just that everything has been more than I've experienced before. Better than anything before and I'm a curious girl who's always taken a male perspective on sex. I'm not the village bicycle. I'm pickier than most, but if I find a ride I want to take—why wait? It doesn't have to be more than sex. Huh, maybe that's the problem? We've been friends for so long it can't be a satisfying fuck? We have to be more than sex? Maybe I'm not ready for this. Damn that Lucy!

Text to Lucy - I'm mad at you

Text from Lucy - What did I do now?

Text to Lucy - You told me about your workbook lesson

Text from Lucy - What happened? You kissed?

Text to Lucy - Yes we kissed.

Text from Lucy - And it was good?

Text to Lucy - No, it wasn't good

Text to Lucy - It was better than good

Text from Lucy - He's the one?

Text to Lucy - I'm not talking about the one

Text from Lucy - What else happened?

Text to Lucy - I slept with him all night and I'm going to do it again

Text to Lucy - Since we were friends, does it mean we can't fuck?

Text from Lucy - Umm

Text from Lucy - Stop being such a guy

Text to Lucy - But...

Text from Lucy - Seriously. You're a girl at heart. Stop hiding.

Text from Lucy - He's the one. Let him be the one.

Text from Lucy - Let it be different this time.

I shove my phone in my pocket without answering again. She's right, but I have no clue how to be a girl. Let him take the lead? I guess? I'll consider it.

Houck

"Looks like it's going well with your friend," Seno laughs.

"Man, when I kiss her she makes me stronger. She's not like anybody else."

He hands me a bat, "Show me how much stronger."

Fuck. Again? I'm not going to argue with him, but there's no way I get brought in to hit. I'm the closer. I stand in ready to hit and everything seems to be moving slower around me. The ball is in focus. The pitch is obvious from the release and the grip the pitcher is using. The spin of the ball out of the two-finger grip and it starts to drop. It's a sinker ball, but it doesn't appear to have much drop on it. I swing my bat hard and connect. The sound is clean and rewarding off my bat, but not as rewarding as the sound coming from behind the dug out. "Woooooo! That's my Super D! Go D!" at the top of her lungs as the ball flies out of the park. The next pitch is a four-seamer straight fastball and I see it coming, straight down the middle of the plate. Smack! Again and I have the power to do anything as the ball lands in the visiting bullpen. "That's my man! Go Super D! Super D!" Everything is clear. I connect to every pitch, hitting six more out of the park during batting practice and being rewarded by Angie's cheering every time. My Super D. My Man. She makes me better, indestructible, tougher, stronger. I'm a superhero for her. I'm her Super D and I want to be hers.

CHAPTER EIGHT

Angie

The game is going great. The Seals are up 7-2 in the 7th inning and D probably won't get to pitch because the team is ahead by more than 3, it's not a save situation. It's still a win. In the 8th inning the wheels come off and the visiting team scores 5, tying the game at 7 with a bases loaded walk and a grand slam. It's ugly and he's warming up in the pen. The game is tied and they don't play all of the closer lights when he comes running in. "Sex Type Thing" rattles the stadium and he's into it. I'm standing on my feet yelling from behind home plate, "Let's do this Super D! You can hold them!" He's ready and the first batter steps into the box. Seno gives the sign and the pitch is straight down the middle at 99 miles per hour, strike one. Second pitch is low, but catches the strike zone for a called strike. Third pitch is challenging the hitter, right down the middle and he swings getting a piece of it and fouling it off. Fourth pitch, a changeup thrown in to throw off the hitter's timing and a called ball. Fifth pitch, 103 miles per hour. Fastball straight down the pipe and the hitter swings and misses. Strike three. One out. The second hitter steps into the box and Seno does his routine of swinging his head from side to side and turning to wave at Sherry. He's funny. He does things to throw off timing and make the hitter's wonder. I wouldn't be surprised if he says things to throw them off, too. Sherry does. Seno gives the sign and D delivers the pitch on the high inside corner for a strike, exactly where the catcher is set up. The second pitch is on fire. A strike clocked at 106 miles per hour and flame graphics run on all the light bars and the big screen. The hitter never saw it coming. Third pitch is a changeup again, the hitter swings and misses. Strike three. Two out. Third hitter digs his cleats in and the pitch is delivered low and inside to push him back away from the plate. Ball one. The second pitch is 102 miles per hour right down the pipe, the hitter swings and misses. The count is one ball and one strike. Third pitch is a fastball down the middle again, this time at 104 miles per hour and the hitter is caught looking. One and two. Fourth pitch and he let's it rip, challenging the hitter. Flames light up the stadium again as he strikes out the side, this time hitting 107 miles per hour. I'm out of my seat screaming for him, "That's my Super D! Way to bring the heat!" He smiles at me as he walks off the mound. He kisses two fingers and points them at me. It's crazy how happy it makes me, but it does. It makes me more than happy and I can't explain it.

The Seals are up to bat in the 9th and they need to score or this game is going into extra innings. The leadoff spot is up and Chase Cross steps into the batter's box hitting the first pitch and getting a base hit. Shortstop Jones Mason is up next and smacks a grounder to the third baseman. He's out at first base, but Cross advances to second. Kris Martin digs into the batter's box intent on knocking it out of the park. He swings at the first pitch and pops it up, caught in centerfield. 2 outs. It's Seno's turn to hit and he takes four straight balls for a walk. The pitcher is in the fifth spot due to a double switch earlier in the game and I watch to find out who they bring in to hit with one out left. Super D is standing there with a bat in the on deck circle waiting for direction. Waiting for the coach to pull him back and put in a hitter, but he doesn't. I'm out of my seat, "Super D! Super D! Super D! Go Super D! Woooooo!" He focuses on me and smiles, the stress of the situation melting away from his face. "Let's do this, D! Woooooo!" Seno is clapping at him from first and Cross has a huge lead off of second. All he needs is a single to bring in Cross and the Seals win with a walk-off. The intensity of the situation is getting the best of me. My whole body is buzzing and I'm anxious for him. I might as well be in the batter's box. The first pitch is delivered and it's a ball outside. The second pitch is high and inside, Sherry and I are both out of our seats yelling at the pitcher. I'm louder than her and that's saying something, "Watch it meat! Don't be throwing at my man!" I don't know what's come over me. Next pitch and it's in slow motion. His grip changes on the bat and his eyes track the ball. He swings and the same sound I heard at batting practice rings through the stadium. I'm screaming again, "OMG! Super D! Wooooo!" I watch the ball sail over the wall in left field. Home run. Seals walk it off with a final score of 10-7. I climb over the seats in front of me to watch him cross home plate at the net and witness his joy as he runs into the scrum of his teammates waiting for him. It's a celebration, and he made it happen. His teammates disperse and he turns to me, kissing two fingers and pointing at me right as they dump a vat of gatorade over his head. He's pumped up and he doesn't care.

He does a quick interview with the on-field reporter, but the whole time he's focused on me. He walks straight to me at the net and gazes at me without speaking.

"You were awesome tonight."

He blushes, "You were cheering for me. Nothing matters as much as you calling me your man. You make me stronger. I ordered dinner in, it might get there before me. I'll be home as soon as I can." He holds my hand on the net and the lightning is back shooting through my body.

"I'll be waiting for you." I smile and he takes off for the clubhouse.

"Nice job," Sherry high-fives me. "You'll see there's nothing better."

I don't doubt her one bit.

CHAPTER NINE

Angie

I get back to his place to find a table for two with candles set up on the balcony. Place settings set out perfectly and a long stemmed red rose sitting on one of the chairs. It's romantic. I run into my room to change into something more appropriate for a date night dinner and thumb through what I've brought with me. I brush out my hair, attempting to get rid of the hat hair I've developed and tie it up into a chignon, a little fancy, it accentuates my bare neck, and hides my hat hair. I throw on the black dress I brought with me along with my strappy black high heels. I add to the ambiance by turning on some music. I skim through his play lists and choose one titled "my heart." The first song is "Angela" by the Lumineers. The elevator opens and a personal chef walks out, going straight to the kitchen with a cart of plates and food. I think it's odd he doesn't say anything until D steps out of the elevator right after him. He's focused on me and walks directly to me in his dark blue jeans and black long-sleeved button up shirt. He's absolutely gorgeous and he slides his arms around me without saying a word. He pulls me against him and holds me there, simply gazing into my eyes. He kisses my cheek and takes my hand, leading me to his balcony. He pulls the chair out for me and pushes me in, handing me the rose from the seat. He pulls the cork on a bottle of champagne like a professional and pours us each a glass.

"You're beautiful and you're all I've ever wanted. I don't know what finally brought us together, but I'm glad it did. To us," he toasts and clinks his glass to mine.

All I can do is giggle. He's an adult who's learned how to do adult things. I missed seeing him grow into being this responsible and respectable adult man. He didn't think I was interested because I've always been able to take care of myself, but in reality he's the same way. Neither of us need someone else. It makes it more special when we choose each other.

We each take a sip of champagne and the bubbles tickle my nose. I play with the rose he gave me, brushing it across my cheek. I'm a teenager again. Everything is new.

Houck

"You never told me why you're visiting me."

"It's silly," She laughs it off.

"Whatever it is, it brought you to me. It brought us together and there's nothing I take more seriously." I have to be completely honest and straight with her. This is Angie.

She stares off into the night sky, "My business partner is getting married. She's taking a pre-marital class at her church with her fiancé and she shares what they learn with me. It's more her way of reviewing and making basic notes for her to have in the future. Last week, she brought me a copy of the workbook page and told me to answer the ten questions." She shifts her focus to me, "Based on my answers she asked me the follow up questions and, basically, it said I should be with you." She takes a breath and continues with her hands flying everywhere, "I didn't believe it. I could've done a quiz in a fashion magazine. It had nothing to substantiate it. I tried to blow it off, completely forget about it, but I couldn't. Lucy told me to visit you and kiss you. She actually kicked me out of the office until I did it. I decided I should at least visit you and spend some time with you, but that was it. Somehow it got us here. It's batshit crazy."

"I need to thank Lucy," he chuckles. "What do you want, Ang?"

"I want you. We're friends, but this is new and the beginning is always exhilarating while you're discovering each other. I don't know what the best way to do this is, but I don't want to lose the excitement. Lucy told me to stop being a guy and let the girl come out."

"I don't want to mess this up and lose you completely."

"What's being together worth to you? It's a risk we have to take. We'll always wonder if we don't."

"Do we take it slow or?" he shakes his head. "We can't start at the beginning and date. We're past that. You already spent the night in my bed. We know each other too well."

"Take the lead and follow your gut. You won't hurt me, and if you do? It'll be worth it. I'll regret it everyday and question if we would've been better together if we don't," her eyes fill with tears, though she's not crying. It's her heart coming out. The girl she hides away behind her facade.

I've wanted her for so long. I can't let myself in any deeper if we won't work. I never want to hurt her. I stare down at my plate and talk, "I need to know if we want the same things. Not now, but in time. Do you want to be married? Have kids? Where do you want to live? What about me being a baseball player and everything that goes with it?"

"I want to have kids if it's with the right man and I don't care where we live or if we get married. All I care is that we're together. I love to watch you play, but I don't know how it'll mesh with my business. I need to figure out all the logistics. It might not be ideal, but I'm sure there's a way."

The chef sets a salad of mixed greens and arugula dressed in balsamic vinaigrette in front of each of us.

I stand up and take her hand, leading her away from the table. "Dance with me," I request softly, placing my other hand on the small of her back. She follows my lead and we sway to "Somebody" by Depeche Mode. Holding her close in my arms, she's all I've ever wanted. She leans her cheek against my chest and wraps her arm around my waist. If I didn't have this shirt on, she'd have her hands on my bare skin like she did this morning. I'd do anything for her to graze my bare skin. I lean down and kiss her. I want to be appropriate, but I can't control my kiss. I've wanted her for too long. It's a 15 year long date that never got to first base until now and fuck me if I'm not going to turn this into a grand slam. I shouldn't, but I find myself kissing her harder and sucking on her lips. Thrusting my tongue into her mouth over and over. She's sucking on my tongue and digging her fingers into my back. Fuck. We're not going to stop. She pulls my shirt out of my jeans and unbuttons it while she's kissing me. I kiss her neck, needing to catch my breath, "Dinner in might have been a bad idea."

"Everything seems about right to me, but I've lost my appetite for food," she bites my neck and nibbles at my ear. "If I was some girl you met, what would you do?"

Fuck! "You're not some girl. I can't fuck you hard and put you away sore."

Angie

"What if I want to be fucked hard? What if I want you to take me and do all the things you want to do to me?" I can't help myself. Lucy said to be a girl, but some things don't change. Maybe someday if it's more than sex. Maybe if I sense something different, something more, like the flutters Lucy talks about in her belly. But, this is what I'm comfortable with. My guy-like perspective. I want to fuck. I bite my lower lip while I stare up into his eyes. No matter what, he's a guy. He can't turn me down.

He searches my eyes, "Is that what you want from me?" His body language changes and he steps away from me, "One hot fuck is not worth losing you. Don't you understand you're more to me? I've wanted you forever. Fuck! I've been in love with you since college. Damn it! I wasn't supposed to say that," he turns away and stares off into the night.

"Say what?" I ask without getting closer to him.

"That's not how you were supposed to find out I love you, okay?"

"You what?"

He turns to me from across his balcony, "I love you, Angie. You weren't supposed to find out because I blurted it out when I was mad. I've known exactly how I would tell you for years and it's too soon to say it. Shit."

"What else do you have planned out? I don't want plans. I want to experience you," I walk toward him. "I want to experience us," I kiss his lips tenderly. "You bring out the girl in me, only you, D." I rest my hand on his chest and wait for a response. I'm not good at this. He doesn't speak. "D? Show me how it's supposed to be. Make me feel like a girl." Still nothing, "I swear

I'm not using you. I don't want to be one of those girls. I don't want to wait. I want you, and I want to be with you—naked.'

"You sound like a guy."

"It's a problem I have. Maybe you can change it."

"I didn't think you had any problems. I thought you were perfect. I still do."

"I'm not perfect. I'm a guy when it comes to sex. I don't get invested. Happy?"

"You need someone to treat you like the woman you are." He turns my head toward him, forcing me to focus on him, "That someone is me, and only me from now on. Do you understand? I promise you, I'll make everything right for you and you'll never want anyone else. But, I don't want even the thought of you ever being with anyone else again. I will always be your next and your last."

I shiver and the thunder in my belly expands throughout my body. "Yes, please."

He scoops me up over his shoulder and walks inside. He calls out to the chef, "Package the meal up for us. We'll be eating later. Thank you." He carries me into his bedroom and shuts the door behind us. He tosses me onto his bed and takes his shirt off, letting it fall to the floor.

I giggle, watching him stand there focused on me.

He smiles, "What are you giggling about?"

"You. You make me excited."

He crawls onto his bed wearing only his jeans and wraps his arms around me, "Hey, beautiful." He gazes into my eyes and presses his lips to mine, soft and tender. I love the sensation of his body, bare skin and hard muscles. I go for the button on his jeans, "Are you sure you want me?"

"Yes. I want all of you." He doesn't stop me. He tugs on my lower lip and groans. He moves his hands over my body and squeezes my ass. I unbutton his jeans and pull the zipper down. I reach in and find him hard in my hand.

"Oh, Angie. Please." His eyes close at my touch.

"D, you should take these jeans off."

His jeans disappear and he's throbbing in my hand, getting harder. I pull him out of his boxer briefs and take a peek. My earlier encounter with his hard-on told me he's above average, but he's better, bigger than I imagined. I'm possessed and have to kiss it. I give it a sweet peck on the tip and he shivers at my intimate contact. I run my hand up and down the length of his shaft, silky and ready to pound nails. I kiss his tip again and swipe my tongue around him, giving him a suck. I want him. I take him into my mouth and have to swallow to get halfway down his huge cock.

"Oh fuck, Angie. This isn't supposed to be first."

I suck on him and take him deeper, licking him and stroking him with my lips. He grabs me around my waist and lifts me up to sit on his chest.

"Tell me you're mine. I want to make you feel what I feel, I want to make you happy. I'll never do anything you don't want."

I pull my dress up over my ass, showing him my red lace panties and suck on him hard.

Suddenly he has both hands kneading my ass, and slides my panties off. "I've wanted you for so long." Gently caressing me along my seam, but not penetrating. He pulls me back toward him and kisses my inner thigh. He kisses my thigh again, open-mouthed and moves closer to my sex. I shiver and he gets closer again, pulling me toward him. I suck on his cock hard as I release him and D takes control. He lifts me at my waist and sits me on the bed beside him. He slowly removes my dress, pulling it over my head and sends it sailing across the room. His eyes settle on my breasts and his hands soon follow, cupping them appreciatively. He unhooks the clasp and bares me to him.

"Anything you want, D. I want to be a girl for you." He

squeezes my breasts, playing with my nipples and kissing each of them. Licking and sucking at my nipples. The way his hands are on me is something I've never experienced before, more than need or want. It pushes the thunder through my body, shaking me to my core with want. He pushes his boxer briefs off and lies naked beside me. He's a gorgeous man, solid muscle everywhere. Classically handsome with his strong jawline, bright shining eyes, and perfect lips. He holds me naked and searches my eyes until he smiles. "What made you smile?"

"I found what I was waiting for," he presses his lips to mine, cherishing me. He pulls back and gazes at me, placing my hands on his chest, "Feel what you do to me?" His heart is pounding in his chest. I kiss his chest and pull his mouth to mine. I nibble on his lips and slide my tongue into his mouth to find his. Sliding my tongue against his until he takes control of the kiss with open-mouthed kisses and I'm suddenly out of breath. I take his hand in mine and hold it to my chest, his eyes light up and he immediately goes back to kissing me. He keeps his hand on my chest wanting to revel in my reaction to him. He's tugging and sucking on my lower lip when the whimper escapes my lips. "Let everything go. I'll take care of you. Let me be the one," he vows soft and sincere. He goes back to kissing me open-mouthed and sucking on my lips. He glides his hand down my body over my hip and stops with his hand on my upper thigh. The anticipation is killing me. He rolls us over. He's on top of me and keeps kissing me. Kissing me as if I'm all he wants and somehow a magic genie has given me to him. I'm drawn into his kiss and focus on his tongue playing with mine. The kiss is everything in my existence or he's found a way to take me to his. I'm not sure which and I don't care. I'm happy to be in the same place and I'm willing to do whatever it takes to get there. Right now, I'd do anything for him. He's the only man who matters. The only thing in my world and I'm revolving around him. How did this happen? Do I need him? He's the one. He stops and stares at my face as he slides his finger inside me. I moan in pleasure as he begins to stroke me. He's still kissing me and holds me tighter against him. He gets hard against my leg. He slides a second finger in and keeps stroking me.

"D, please."

"Sshhhhhh. I'm taking care of you. I want to make you happy. I promise I'll give myself to you, all of me, heart, soul and dick."

I writhe at his hand, "Oh, D. Fuck." I'm wound up and ready to go, but he won't let me. He keeps stroking his fingers in and out.

"You're so hot and wet, baby. Do you want more?"

"Yes. D, I want to come." I reach for my sex and clutch at his hand stroking me.

He takes my hand and shows me how wet I am, then sucks my fingers clean, "Mmmmm." I want to touch myself, but he takes my hand away while he draws a line of kisses down my body directly to my sex. He kisses my thigh and gives me a nibble up even higher on my thigh. He licks my seam where his fingers are sliding in and out of my heat.

I cry out a noise I've never heard before, uncontrolled and full of desire. I beg, "Please," and wonder who has taken control of me. Is this the effect he has on me? When did he become a baseball playing sex god?

He settles his mouth at my clit, kissing me there as if he's making out with me and it's all it takes. My body, ready to explode, spools up even tighter with his added tenderness and I'm lost.

I'm falling in the darkness and I can't catch myself. There's no ledge to grab onto. No safety net to catch me at the bottom. There's no bottom, it's an infinite fall. I'm screaming out to D, but I'm not sure if he can hear me or if I'm actually making any sound. He stops stroking me and now I'm being pulled somewhere.

He kisses my lips, "I need you. I'm going to have you now, baby. You want me?"

I answer him in a shaky tone, "Yes."

"That's what I want to hear." He rolls me over on my belly and spreads my legs, leaving them hanging off the end of his bed. "I want you doggie style on the bed now." His words are unexpected and I don't respond. "I said now." I giggle. "You must want to be spanked." He lays his hard cock on my ass, "Feel how big and heavy I am? I'm going in you and I'm going to slam you hard from behind until you can't walk, until you do everything I want. Until you beg me for more after you've already come more times than you have ever come in one night before." He rubs his hand across my ass, "Such a sweet ass to spank until it's red. Then fucking you and smacking into it over again and again. I can't wait. Okay, bad girl." Is he kidding with this? What game is he playing? He smacks my ass firmly, over and over. I'm squirming at the sting and move quickly in between spanks to get in position for him. "Have you had enough? All you've done is cry out my name asking for more." There's no way? Then again, I didn't get up and run away. "Are you ready, baby? I'm giving you my Super D." He holds his cock with both hands and lines it up, rubbing the tip against my entrance. He has to push to get in, he's huge.

I scream out at the intensity and how much he's stretching me. His pure size pushing into me relentlessly.

"You feel me, baby?"

"Uh-huh," I'm finally able to respond.

"Do you feel full? You should see how big your hole is stretched for me."

"Very full," still limited in my speech.

"Trust me. You're not full yet. That's only my tip."

He slams into me all at once and I scream out again as he slams into my wall. His girth penetrating all the way into me.

"Come on, baby, I need to fit all the way in. There's still a couple inches. You can do it. I want to mash my body against yours when I slam into you." He's in deep and pushes further, "Almost."

"Oh. Oh," I can't function. I can't put words together. All there is, is him.

"Ang, you need to be able to take me the whole way if you want me to fuck you hard. It's what you want, right? It's what you asked for and I'll always give you what you ask for. He slams me over and over, harder and harder until he's smashed up against me. "Yeah, you're my girl. Do you like it, baby?"

"Yes."

"I knew you would. Do you want more?"

"Anything for you, D."

He pulls out and rolls me over to my back, "Do you mean it? Anything for me?"

"Yes."

"Is it what you want? Fucked hard and fast?"

"Anything to make you happy, D."

"It's not what I want. I want to take care of you and love you and be naked together. I did it because you wanted to be fucked and you should experience getting fucked. I'll do anything for you, even fuck you hard when you need it."

Breathless, "D? Fuck me hard and make me come. I'll be yours, anything you want for the rest of the night." I'm not sure what's come over me, but I have to see it through. This is an experience I can't pass up, I need him to fuck me. I want him to be in control.

He doesn't speak. He simply stares at me. I move back to the edge of the bed and get on all fours with my ass in the air. "Do you want me or not, D?"

He gets up and stands behind me at the foot of the bed, his hands on my hips, "It's what you want. I'll always give you what you want." He rubs his tip in my wetness and slams into me all at once. "If you want it, I should enjoy it. Fuck me." He slams into me over and over. I'm screaming out in pleasure on every stroke. "All me, Ang. Remember, nobody else can do this for you. Only Super D."

It's hard and fast and so fucking intense. I start to move with him, moving in time to meet his strokes and slamming us together. He's huge, my head hanging down and I watch him slamming me from behind. He's hard and his extra thick head... he's amazing massaging me inside, and anchoring him inside me. "Oh, D. Fuck. More. Don't stop, Super D!"

"Anything you want," his breath ragged. Did I send him over the edge? He pounds into me harder and faster. His fingers grip my hips tight and dig into the flesh. He holds on while we get lost together, "Angie, baby. I'm close. I need you. Hard and fast and I'm done. Tell me to come inside. I always wear a condom, but this is you and..."

"Anything you want for the rest of the night. I'm yours, D. Your call."

"Fuck me." He strokes into me harder and harder, his body tensing and cock rigid, "You're on birth control?"

"No. Your call."

He doesn't hesitate. "Come for me, Angie," he whispers. "I want you to come with me." He leans over me and cups my breasts, holding on while he fucks me. "You're mine," he possessively shoves himself into me as far as he can.

"Oh, D! Now."

He slams me harder than before and I come violently around his huge cock, "Oh, fuck." His pattern changes slightly, "Inside, baby. Coming inside you, Angie."

"Doug! Doug!" I cry out as I spiral out of control. The

thunder turns to a hurricane of need and emotions and I already want him again.

He wraps his arms around me tight and kisses my back, "I've got you, Angie. I'll always take care of you." He shoves in hard a couple times, then moves slower, but doesn't stop. "Are you okay for more?"

"Anything for you, whatever you want all night, Super D," my voice is softer, more feminine.

He pulls out of me slowly and I roll over onto my back, giggling like a school girl. "That's a happy sound," he says and crawls up next to me. He kisses me tenderly and searches my eyes. Wrapping his arms around me, "I love you and I'll always give you what you want, the way you want it. But, sometimes I want to love you. You're not on birth control? You let me come inside, I want to come inside you all night. Fuck, I want to come inside every time from now on. You're where I belong."

"I love how you make me a girl. I don't want to be in charge when I'm with you, I want you to be in control. I want you in control of everything. I don't want to make decisions. I want you to take care of me. I want you to love me and sometimes fuck me, because I might be bad," I smile at him. "You want to keep coming inside me? Your call." There's no way I deny this man anything. Yes, he's truly Super D, but it's more. He's Doug. He's always been there for me. What took me so long to discover he's the one. Yes, it's true, he's the one. He'll do anything for me and always will, but he's taken my heart from me in trade. No, I'm giving him my heart and my body willingly. I'm his.

CHAPTER TEN

Houck

I want to love her. I always want to love her. I bow down at her sex and kiss it, licking her clit until she shakes. I move up to her body, rubbing my tip in her wetness and push in slow while I kiss her, "Isn't this better, baby?" I get completely buried inside her and wrap my arms around her, moving slowly. She doesn't answer me and I want her to come around me again. I sit up on my knees and take in our connection. I push into her until we're completely one, "Do you want to touch yourself?" She reaches toward her clit and I take her hand, making her grasp how big I am at our connection. Her hand on my cock is almost enough to set me off. I caress her swollen clit and she shivers. "It's okay. I've got you." I rub it and she implodes around me, squeezing my cock. I lean over her moving in and out slowly while she comes, "I love you, baby." I kiss her neck and wrap my arms around her, "I've got you." She's not with me. I hold her and wait. Her breathing is heavy and her heart is beating as strong as mine. She's amazing around me and our heat is crazy. I push and pull with her tight around me and I'm done at simply the idea of being in Angie. I'm throbbing hard and she's still contracting around me while I come. How is this better with her? Fuck! I can't keep coming inside her. Too late now, she's getting everything and I want her to have it.

I'm happier than I've ever been because I have her with me. Kissing her, holding her, getting inside her, all things I could only imagine and now she's here in my bed, willing to give me anything I want. She left it up to me to make the decisions and I didn't take care of her. She told me she's not on birth control and I came in her anyway. Here's the kicker, I'm going to come inside her every chance I get and I'm going to come hard. What the hell am I thinking? Shit! What did I do? We're not married. We're not engaged. We're not even dating. We don't live together. Shit, we don't even live on the same side of the country. My stupid ass makes a decision that has her living alone and finding herself pregnant. What decision does she make if I'm not there? There's no way for me to have a clue. She could keep it to herself and never say a word. She could hide from me and I'd never get to talk to her again. Fuck. I'm in love with her and she's going to leave.

I still have her in my arms when my mouth takes control, "Stay here with me."

"I'm staying right here with you all night, D. I told you I'm yours tonight."

I take a deep breath, "I meant don't go home. This should be your home. This should be your bed. You should be with me."

"D, I..."

I don't want her reasons for why she can't be here or how this is just a weekend or we need time to make sure this is what we want. It doesn't matter and I've had a long time to contemplate it. I'm not giving her up. "We can hire somebody to pack your belongings up and ship them here for you. We can set up a virtual office for you. I can go to your place at the All-Star Break and help you get packed and moved. I want you here with me. I want you to be mine. I want to take care of you." My internal voice is at full speed and ready to express my desires. *I want to get you pregnant. I want you to be my wife. I don't care what order it happens in.* Then in a soft voice, "I want you cheering for me at every game and screaming out my name in our bed. I only want to give Super D to you." Fuck she makes me crazy.

She places her hand on my chest and searches my eyes, "Douglas Houck, you need to get a grip. You know me. You know I consider everything and make calculated decisions. This whole weekend is outside my comfort zone." She stops talking and her expression softens. I open my mouth to speak and she places two fingers over my lips to keep me quiet. I kiss her fingers and wait for her to continue. "I'm not sure what to say. I guess, I don't let anyone else have control or make decisions for me. But you? I want you to be in control. I don't have to think when I'm with you because you'll take care of me. You always have. You make me feminine, more of a woman. Nobody does that. I think I need you."

She hasn't caught up to me yet. She doesn't know she loves me. I don't need her to say the words, her eyes have already shown me. I need to love her and prove it's real.

Houck

I wrap my arms around her, kissing her glorious lips. I spread her legs with mine and lie in between them while we kiss. Our kiss grows hotter by the second, I push into her and pull a squeal from her lips. Slowly, I bury myself deep inside her and watch her face as she experiences me. Opening her mouth and dragging her teeth across her lower lip. Her hands grasp at the headboard. Whimpers and cries come from her sweet lips. I claim her mouth while I move slowly inside her, needing all of her to be mine, "I love you. Please be mine." My words are unstable in the pit of my stomach. It's what I hope for, more than asking her for anything. Expressing my love for her is something I never dreamed I'd be able to do and here I am, declaring the words to her with all my heart. She moves her hands across my back and digs her fingers in. I explore her neck with my lips, loving her tenderly.

"Oh, D," she releases on a sexy sigh. "There's only you."

"Good, I don't want to share you."

"No, you don't understand. Everything else in the world is gone. It's only you."

Fuck me, "Only me. All of me inside you?"

"Yes, D. Super D."

"My lips on yours kissing you, kissing your neck?"

"Uh-huh, and your words, oh... honest to my heart."

"Everything I do or say will always be true. I've been waiting for you." I keep moving slowly and she's amazing around me. "Feel me move for you? I want to stay right where I am forever." Her hands glide over my body, a lustful caress, and she palms my ass with both hands. She starts to move with me, responding to me as I stroke into her. It's pushing me, "I want to go slow, Ang. Let me love you. Can't you feel what we are together?" She must. This attraction and heat we have is undeniable. She must sense it, it can't just be me.

Angie

I want to move with him. My body has to move with him and meet his actions. I need to. I need him. Super D makes me lose my mind, huge and hard. Nothing from my past compares. If I'm being honest, it's more than the Super D. It's superior in every way, but mostly it's him. I can't close my eyes without visions of him, he speaks and I'm overcome by his devoted words. When he declares his love for me, I believe him with every cell of my being. This easy sex is making it undeniable and sending his love for me to every part of me. It's a slow burn and he's pushing me closer with every delectable stroke. How can I want him this bad when I already have him? "It's so much," escapes my lips.

He's at my ear, "Do you want me to stop?"

"No, don't stop. Never stop. Love me, D."

"Always." He starts to grind against me on every stroke and I'm lost to the darkness without warning, hit unexpectedly by my orgasm.

I scream out his name and thread my fingers into his hair, holding him at my collarbone where he's kissing me. He keeps moving at his steady, easy pace.

"I love it when you scream out my name. I'll have to have you a couple more times before I'm done tonight."

Fuck me. My emotions respond, "Yes, please. Anything for you." I'm still coming around his hard love, his strokes pushing me further.

"You're so tight around me. You make me want to come now."

It's getting hotter and he moves his hands to my head, holding me where he wants me and kissing me. His movements are consistent and deliberate, but his kiss pushes forward. I'm completely his, here for his every whim. He nibbles at my lips and licks me from the base of my neck to my mouth. It's hard to breathe. My senses are all overcome and I can't concentrate on anything, only D. The friction building between us with the kiss. Him tugging on my lips, sucking on my tongue, playing with my hair, completely in control. It's never been this way. I'm always in control.

"You don't need to be in control with me. You're my woman and I belong to you. The only thing I need to do in my life is make you happy and give you pleasure. Until now, all I've done is practice for you. I'm here to take care of you." He claims my mouth, kissing me hard and needy. I wrap my legs around him. "Oh, fuck. Hold on." I squeeze him with my legs around his waist. "Hands, too." I grab onto him around his neck. He sits up on his knees, taking me with him as I cling to him. His hands are splayed across my back, supporting me as he slides in and out of me. "Trust me," he requests and I let go of his neck. He leans me away from him, holding me in his strong arms and focuses on me as he smiles. It's a stretch with my legs snugly around him. He pushes into me completely, our bodies mashed together at our connection. He slides me back and forth on his hard cock, stroking himself with my body.

"Oh, D," I let my head hang back in pleasure.

He moves me faster and the friction grows quickly, "I want..."

The thunder inside me is rumbling and ready to release. I'm full and sated, yet want more of him when he moves me even faster and slams me on his huge cock over and over. His cock becomes more rigid and he's throbbing inside me as he pushes in as deep as he can get. "Please don't stop," I beg uncontrollably.

He growls, "I love how you want more. I'm ready for you." He lays me back down on the bed and goes back to his easy pace. He pats my thigh and he grabs my legs as I release them from around him. He's still hard and wanting more. He leans into me, spreading my legs and finding my deep place easily. I whimper. "Do you like me deep inside you, Angie?"

I nod, "I love it, D." He leans in to kiss me, getting even deeper, "More."

"Soon, baby." He sits back up, "You're beautiful." He strokes into me slow, "There's still more for you." He circles my clit, teasing as he closes in on it, and he has me tightly wound. He strokes into me harder and finally works my clit. The thunder wins and I'm coming hard around him in darkness. I'm lost again, each time seeming to be further gone and more his.

"D! Fuck. D!" He grabs my legs and bends me in half, pounding into me hard and I come again instantly. "D! Fuck, Super D! So deep." I scream out of my mind being pulled from my darkness and suddenly warm all over.

He's out of breath, "So deep, baby. You're my girl. I'm coming with you." Suddenly slamming into me even harder, "Fuck. Fuck! Angie, I need you." I reach for him blindly in my state of bliss and we move together. My hands are on his back, holding him while his warm cum fills me. Our hearts pound together, hot and out of control, "I love you, baby."

"I love you, too," the words escape my lips without even thinking. They've been hiding there, behind my lips and captured by my left-brain. Maybe I've loved him for years. He kisses me and I can feel the grin on his face broaden.

CHAPTER ELEVEN

Angie

I wake up in the middle of the night hungry with D on top of me and I've got to pee. His arms are wrapped around me. I love it. I start to slide out from under him and he grabs my hand, so I can't leave. He immediately locks his fingers with mine and that's all it takes to bring the thunder back. "I'm not leaving. I need to pee." He opens his eyes and gazes at me full of concern as he releases my hand. I stand up and start walking to the bathroom.

"I always use a condom, but I didn't with you. I'm not apologizing. I know what I did and I didn't pull out. You're perfect. I love you and it felt like the right thing to do. When I'm in you, I want to stay there."

My back to him, I close my eyes as his cum runs down my thigh. Last night is blurry. I remember he's truly the Super D and he showed me he can take control, but wants more. It's one night, I'm sure it won't be a problem. There have been a couple broken condoms in my past and they worked out okay. I could get a Plan

B pill, but I don't want to. What does that mean? I don't want to? I pee and find I'm cleaning up more from last night than I thought was possible.

Angie

His alarm goes off and he talks to me with his arms around me warm and protective, "The last thing I want to do this morning is leave you in my bed alone. I have to get ready and go to the stadium. No BP today and I understand if you don't want to get out of bed in time to go to the game. You don't have to." He kisses my forehead, "I love you, my beautiful girl."

I groan and don't open my eyes, grabbing his pillow to snuggle with. He goes about his morning getting ready and I go back to sleep. But as soon as the penthouse is empty, my brain won't stop replaying everything that happened last night. It's when I remember I told him he could do whatever he wanted, I was his and he chose to come inside me every time. I didn't care last night when it was happening and he was in control. Fuck, I love it when he's in control. He wants me to stay here with him and he wants to get me pregnant. He loves me.

Text to Lucy - How's business?

Text from Lucy - What happened?

Text to Lucy - Just checking in… Geez

Text from Lucy - You know I'm not working. It's Sunday.

Text to Lucy - You need me back at the office?

Text from Lucy - I'm Wonder Woman, I can do it all.

Text from Lucy - Run a business, generate new clients, and plan a wedding at the same time.

Text from Lucy - Piece of cake when you have a magic lasso.

Text to Lucy - I wasn't trying to extend my getaway

My phone rings and it's Lucy, "What?"

"Hello my missing partner. What's going on there? First, is he the one or not?"

"He's the one."

"Um, really? I mean, I knew he was, but you agreed too easily."

"I love him. He loves me. He kisses like sin. He's hung like a donkey. He wants me to stay."

"Hhhhmmmm, you had guy sex."

"Maybe, okay yes. I had guy sex, but it was only at first and I…"

"Finish your sentence. I hate it when you do this. Use your damn words."

"I like it when he's in control. I love his hands on me. He makes me feminine," I surprise myself with my words and feminine tone.

"You need to come home now. You sound like a girl. You're obviously ill. What did you do with Angie?"

"That's what I was afraid of. It's him, not me. I'm coming home."

"Wait. Is he what you want?"

"I'd like to stay in his bed and never leave."

"I'm sure he'd provide you room and board for your services "

"Not funny!"

"Sorry, it was too easy."

"Where's your manpiece?"

"I stayed home, didn't go to his place this weekend."

"You haven't spent a week without him in... ever."

"He may have pissed me off and turned into a stupid man."

"Passing or are we going to talk about it?"

"The pre-marital course is working out much better for you than it is for me."

"Sorry."

"Me, too. Could be a deal breaker."

"Pick me up at the airport tonight?"

"I'll be there."

She needs me. I need to get my head straight. I need to go home. Tears roll down my face. I'm not one of those women who cry at everything. I can come back in a few days. I'm not leaving him forever. Shit. I need to tell him I'm leaving. He's not going to like it.

Text to D - Do you have a few minutes before the game?

Text from D - I'll find you pregame behind home plate

Text to D - Somewhere more private maybe?

Text from D - What do you have in mind?

Text to D - I need to talk to you.

Text to D - I like your idea better

I get dressed and pack while I wait for him to respond. I hear the elevator close and turn around to find him standing in the doorway behind me.

"Where are you going? Tell me you're moving into my bedroom," D waits for an answer.

"That's what I need to talk to you about. Lucy needs me back at the office to help her with some drama." I walk toward him and reach my arms up around his neck, "I'm going home to take care of business and I'll be back. I'm not leaving you. I don't want you to get the wrong idea. I'm yours. No other guys for me. Only you, D."

"Wait until after the game and I'll go with you. I'm off tomorrow and don't have to report in until noon on Tuesday."

"This will take a few days to fix and part of the problem is her fiancé. Having you there probably won't help."

"Are you sure it's work? Not me?"

"Lucy needs me. She can't run the business by herself and deal with her personal drama at the same time." I take a deep breath, "I need to get my head straight and get the logistics figured out."

"Please don't leave."

"I promise I'll be back as soon as I can. Hopefully I'll be back in four or five days." I caress his cheek, "I love you, D."

He smiles at me, "I love you, too." He takes my hands in his, "Okay, we're together and you'll come back to me or I'll go to you, whatever we have to do. We'll call and text everyday."

"Yes we will. We have most days since we met."

He lifts me up and hugs me, "I have to get back before I'm missing."

Silent tears stream down my cheeks, I hug his neck and talk into his ear, "Play hard and win, I'll be watching every game. Tell Carter I need a permanent access card ready for me when I get back. I can't believe it took me so long to find you. You're the one. I'll be back to you soon."

He sets me down on my feet and walks into the other room. He comes back to me, "I don't like not having enough time to do what I want to do. I want you to live here, take the key with you. This is your place, too." He kisses me goodbye and he's not happy about it. I'm not either. He turns and as he's running to the door, "I'm going to make you my wife someday. You know that, right?"

"You make me happy, D."

He's smiling when the elevator door closes, but it's as fake as mine. Why am I doing this? I need to get back to the office and help Lucy. Some space will be a good thing. I can do this.

Houck

I hate that she's leaving. She isn't supposed to be leaving yet. I should have at least another day. I have things I wanted to do. I wanted to put the key to my place on a nice key ring before I gave it to her. I wanted to buy a piece of jewelry for her, so she could wear it and remember me. I want her to have me with her. I stop in at Carter's office on my way back in and have a seat.

He looks up from his desk, "What can I help you with today?"

"Angie's gone for a few days, can you get a permanent access card ready for her?"

"No problem. Anything else?"

"Can you get a key ring engraved for her and delivered to her at her office tomorrow with some flowers? A nice sterling silver or something, engraved with D loves Ang. Long-stemmed red roses, not the cheap ones. At least a dozen of them."

"I'll get on it right now."

"Thanks," I get up and go work out, trying to get my mind off it. She said she's coming back, she's not leaving me. Last night was crazy. She loves me. Everything is fine. I'll talk to her tonight. I need to focus on the game.

I watch the game from the bullpen and get stretched out. I did more than I should've last night, I need to make up for it. It was more than worth it. It would be worth it everyday. The game is going slow, mostly because I have her on my mind and she's not here. I'm watching the score and I doubt I get called in to pitch. Seals win 9-4, no need for a closer.

> Text to Angie - Thinking about you. Message me when you land.

Angie

> Text to D - Landed. Thought about you the whole flight home
> Text from D - Your flight to San Diego is your flight home
> Text to D - I know. I'll be home to you soon, D.
> Text to D - Lucy's picking me up, I'll call later

Lucy pulls up and I put my luggage in her hatchback. I hop in the passenger seat, "Hi, thanks for picking me up."

She simply stares at me, "Who are you and what did you do with Angie?"

"What are you talking about?" I laugh.

"You have a grin plastered on your face that I've never seen before and your voice is all light and breezy. Are you actually happy? It's a new look on you. I hope it doesn't affect the logical side of your brain. I need that part for business."

"I haven't changed. I was only gone a few days. I do have some things to talk to you about. But first, take me home and tell me about the potential deal breaker with your stupid man."

On the drive to my third floor apartment, Lucy tells me all about her fiancé and his inability to compromise. She finally gets to the things she won't compromise on, primarily other women.

Apparently, the weekends together because they live two hours apart hasn't been enough. He's been spending the night with other women when they're not together. To quote Lucy, "He said it doesn't matter. It's in a whole different zip code." She's not a happy camper, but better to find out now. She's already made her decision and she's done with him. Which I figure is her being tough to get through it, until she giggles at an alert on her phone.

"What's that about?"

"Oh, this? Nothing," she giggles some more.

"It doesn't look like nothing."

"I figured the quickest way to get over it would be to move on. I joined this dating app. These guys are fun and some of them are cute."

I shake my head at her, but if it helps her get over the jerk then I'm fine with it. It's much better than helping her pick up the pieces and having her be a complete mess. We agree to sit down and discuss business tomorrow.

I get unpacked and start the laundry. If I'm doing this, I need to be ready. I've been considering the logistics and a plan I need to talk to D about. He's probably not going to be a fan, but it makes sense. I can't believe I'm doing this. Am I moving to the other side of the country for a man? For the Super D? It's all for Doug.

I call him, and he answers on the first ring, "Hey, beautiful. I miss you."

I giggle, "Don't be silly. I just left today." I pick on him, but it's the truth. I get warm all over simply hearing his voice over the phone, "I miss you, too."

"When are you coming home?"

"Discussing it with Lucy tomorrow, when we handle the business drama. What do you think about me keeping my apartment here and staying here when you're on road trips? Not permanently, but I'll need to be here sometimes for business and it'll help Lucy be okay with my move. Then we can figure out everything else in the offseason, maybe you can help me finish moving then? It's only five months."

"You'll be here with me when I'm home?"

"That's the idea. There may be minor schedule snafus, but in general we'd come and go on the same days. I might not need to go every time you do and I've been hoping I might get to go on a road trip with you," I smile at the idea of road tripping like a baseball groupie.

"It's better to wait until the offseason, as long as you'll be here. It'll be six months, Seno says we're going to the series this year. Plan on being booked for post-season and spending October with me."

I love the confidence and how the team believes it's their year. The way they play, it wouldn't surprise me. "I can't wait to spend post-season with you!" I have tears in my eyes again, softly, "D, are we crazy?"

"I'm crazy in love with you. Come home soon, baby."

CHAPTER TWELVE

Angie

Monday

Lucy agrees with my plan to move to San Diego half the time and hopes I will find us more clients there. I left out how I'll be moving there full-time in the off-season. Things change. I may need to be here some for business still.

The office drama isn't bad. Dealing with the sales end of things isn't Lucy's strong suit. She's going to have to get better at it. I spend most of the day on the phone with clients and schedule a couple meetings for later in the week. D's going to hate it, but business is business. I need to get better at using my virtual office and contacting clients through the internet and phone instead of walking into their office anyway. It would give me more time if I wasn't driving between clients.

Lucy carries in a crystal vase of long stemmed red roses while I'm on a call and sits there in front of my desk waiting for me to get off the phone. There's at least two dozen dark velvety red roses. I hang up the phone and the smile grows on my face. "They came with this fancy blue box. Open it!" I take the card from the flowers and open it.

Angie—You mean more to me than you know. I'm going to show you how much you mean to me everyday. I can't wait to have you back in my arms. I love you.—D

"What the hell? You're doing it again! That happy smile," Lucy snatches the card from my fingers. She reads the card and shakes her head, "What'd he do to you?"

She tosses the box to me and I open it to find a key ring with a shiny silver heart shaped tag. It's engraved with D loves Ang. There's a note in the box and it reads "Key to my heart and my home. Love you, Ang."

I send D a picture of the flowers and the key ring with a thank you and heart emojis. I get a response of heart emojis back.

"Seriously?" Lucy walks around behind me to be nosey over my shoulder. "Fine, it's sweet."

"He gave me a house key before I left yesterday. You should see his place."

"You mean your new place?"

Huh, "Yes." I try to maintain my smile, but I can't. There's no way. I show Lucy photos of D and tell her about the photo I found on his nightstand. "Did I tell you I live in a penthouse now?" I laugh at the whole thing. This is my life.

———

Angie

My phone rings about 10pm, "Hello?"

"I wish you were with me today."

"I do, too. The roses are beautiful and I put my keys on the key ring you sent. Thank you."

"You deserve more," I can hear his smile through the phone.

"Lucy is on board with me moving. I have client meetings on Thursday. I'll be back on Friday."

"Can't you meet with your clients sooner and come home to me?"

"I need time to pack anyway. I'm moving in. I need to bring my stuff, right?"

"Alright, I get it. Clothes don't pack themselves. Pack up boxes of whatever you want to bring with you and I'll get them shipped for you. There's two walk-in closets in the master bedroom, one of them is empty and waiting for you. I'll be patient, I've waited fifteen years and it's only a few days." His voice changes, lower and raspy, "I love you, Ang. Now that I have you, I never want to be away from you."

Tuesday

I meet Lucy for lunch and go to a couple clients. I spend half the day packing and surveying my apartment, considering what should go and what should stay. Where did all this crap come from? I pack up most of my clothes and shoes I won't be wearing this week. I toss my favorite blanket in a box, along with my photos, and things I've collected following D over the years. Everything else can wait or go with me on the plane.

Text from Carter - Working on your access card. Please send me a current photo.

I send him a quick selfie and send it to D while I'm at it.

Then I get a link, with access to the game live or whenever I want.

Text from Carter - West Coast night games can be hard for
East Coast fans ;)
Text to Carter - Thank you
Text from D - Hey, beautiful :)
Text to D - Hi, handsome ;)

He sends me a selfie in front of his locker in the clubhouse.

Text from D - How's packing?
Text to D - I'm done packing my initial boxes. I have eight
boxes ready to go.
Text from D - I'll get them picked up and shipped, your stuff
will be here waiting for you on Friday.
Text from D - I'll call after the game tonight.
Text to D - :)

I watch the game live and fall asleep before it's over. I'm woken up by my phone ringing, "Hello?"

"Hi, baby. I woke you up. I'm sorry."

"Don't be. I was waiting for you to call. I like to hear your voice. How was the game?" My voice is sweet and it's all because of him.

"We won. I slammed the door with three strikeouts in the ninth inning to hold the score to 4-3 Seals."

"Keep it up and stay focused. I can't wait for October baseball with you. I'll watch the end of the game in the morning."

"Go back to sleep, Ang. I'll see you Friday. I love you."

Wednesday

The boxes I packed get picked up while I'm watching D get the save in last night's game and trying to get motivated for the day. I'm spending the day in the office getting my desk cleaned up and organized, making sure I have everything prepared that I need to work with from San Diego. I might need a desk when I get there. Nah, I'll work from the table on the balcony. It's gorgeous out there and I love the warm sun.

Sitting in my office, I find myself daydreaming while I stare at my roses. He loves me and I doubt anyone else ever has. More importantly, I love him and it's not lust. Everyday I'm away I miss him more.

Lucy walks into my office and looks me up and down, "What are you doing now?"

"It's a day game today."

"You're sitting at your desk watching the game and wearing a baseball jersey. Have you looked at yourself? Where's your office attire?"

"Some things are more important," slips from my lips without a thought. Shit. Try to cover it up, "I have issues, Luc. You know what it's like. Especially at the beginning, in the honeymoon stage." I show her the selfie he sent me, hoping my hunk might buy me some understanding.

"I guess you can do what you want. You're one of the bosses."

I smile in victory, "Thank you."

I hear Sherry yelling when Seno comes up to bat. I want to be there to cheer for D. Seals won 9-2, no closer needed today.

I get home, counting down the hours until I leave for San Diego. I find a Thursday night flight and book it. I send the confirmation to him via text and my phone rings.

"Do you like flying on Thursday nights?"

"I guess. I wanted the flight that would get me to you soonest."

"I love it. I'll be there to pick you up."

"I'm counting on it. Going to bed early, I have a long day tomorrow. Love you, D."

Thursday

I wake up Thursday morning and I'm not rested. I get up and do what I have to do anyway. I meet with my clients and handle business, spending two hours on the road and a couple more in the office. Lucy is starting to freak out and I'm already anticipating the D thunder. It's an unstable situation. We hit happy hour and she follows me home, ready to give me a ride to the airport.

Text from flyaway - Your scheduled flight has been delayed

Fuck. I start to search for details and...

Text from flyaway - Your flight has been canceled
Text from flyaway - Please contact us to reschedule your
flight. We're sorry for any inconvenience.

I check for available flights and the next one is tomorrow at 10am.

Text to D - Flight rescheduled to tomorrow.
Text to D - I hate this. Call me after the game.

CHAPTER THIRTEEN

Angie

I wake up Friday morning when Lucy is banging on my door, "Are we going to the airport today or not?"

Why is she yelling? I open my eyes. Why is the room spinning? I yell out, "Lucy, come in. Use your key."

My door opens, "Angie?"

"In my bedroom."

"Open your eyes and get up. You've got a flight and Super D waiting for you."

Tears stream down my face, "The room spins when I open my eyes. What do I do? Help me here!"

"You look warm and a bit green," she checks my forehead. "You definitely have a fever. Where's your phone?"

"Nightstand."

She picks up my phone and dials. The voice on the other end comes through clear, "Hey, I've been worried about you, beautiful."

"Why thank you, but this isn't beautiful. Well, I'm beautiful but I'm not your beautiful. This is Lucy and I'm putting you on speaker. First, it's nice to finally talk to you, I've heard a lot about you and I'm happy you have finally found each other. Only a little bit jealous."

"Where is she? She didn't answer my call last night. Is she okay?"

"I'm right here, D."

Lucy takes control, "She'll be fine, but she's not getting on a plane today. She may not be getting on a plane for a few days. She has an ear infection or something. She's dizzy and has a fever. I've got her taken care of on this end."

"Baby, are you okay?"

"The room spins when I open my eyes and my head hurts. Don't worry about me. I'll be fine. Play hard and I'll be there as soon as I can. I'm sorry, D."

"Don't worry, I'll take care of her."

"Lucy, please send me a text. I need your number. Thanks for taking care of my girl. I wish I could be there to take care of her myself."

"D, go play ball. I love you."

"Love you, too, babe."

Lucy chimes in, "You two make me sick, bye." She disconnects the call. "Fine, I like him. You can keep him. But, you heard me and I'm not kidding, you're stuck here for a few days. Go back to sleep. I'll check on you in a bit."

CHAPTER FOURTEEN

Angie

I wake up Monday afternoon, finally coherent and not spinning. I sit up and grab my phone. I lost three days.

Text from D - Been in contact with Lucy for updates, didn't want to wake you up.
Text from D - Hope you're better soon. Call me when you can. Love you, Ang. I always have and I always will.

I call him immediately, and he answers, "She lives!"

"Yes, I'm alive. I miss you."

"I miss you more. I think about you all the time. I always have, but now it's different. You're real and what I want isn't a fantasy anymore. I need more than one night with you. Please don't change your mind and stay there."

"I'm not changing my mind. I want to be with you, D."

"Your boxes are already here. The team is off on Thursday, but it's a travel day. I'm on a two week road trip starting on

Thursday. Don't rush and fly out here. Relax and get better. Stay and work or pack or whatever you want. We'll be together soon. I wish I wasn't going on a long road trip. I love you, Ang."

Angie

I spend the next couple weeks watching every Seals baseball game and wearing my Super D jersey to the office for day games. Lucy laughs at me for yelling at D when he's playing, but I don't care. She took a video of me doing it and didn't tell me. I had no idea until D told me she sent it to him and he loved it. The office is tighter, cleaner, and running better than it ever has. Every room in my apartment has been gone through from top to bottom, sorted, cleaned, and reorganized. I miss D. I've done everything I can to keep my mind occupied and be productive. He's expecting me on Friday and he should be home late Thursday night. I can't wait anymore, I'm going a day early to get unpacked and be there waiting for him when he gets home.

CHAPTER FIFTEEN

Angie

I get off the plane in sunny San Diego and get an Uber home. Home. Interesting, it is home. I take my luggage up the elevator and I'm home when the doors open. I immediately go out on the balcony and take a selfie, texting it to D.

Text to D - I'm home and waiting for you

Text from D - I wish I was home with you. See you tonight.

I use every minute of time until he gets home, getting unpacked and organizing my closet. It's huge. There's a spot for every single pair of my shoes, hangers for skirts, pants, even a longer area for dresses. There's a built in dresser, even a velvet-covered ottoman to sit on. I lay my favorite blanket out over the ottoman and put my box of D memorabilia on top of the dresser. One of the nightstands is empty, I claim it setting my auto-graphed books up neatly and plugging in my gaggle of electronic devices. I get rid of the empty boxes and hide my suitcases in the back of my closet. I'm home. It's perfect.

Houck

I'm almost home and I can't wait to see Angie. The last three weeks have been worse than the fifteen years I waited for her. It's not her fault or mine, it's the way it is. Neither of us have talked about the night we spent together. Maybe we don't need to. There was a connection, and now that it's been made we can't go back. It was special. It always will be special with us.

I get home and it's dark, "Angie?" The light's on in our bedroom. I walk in to find her sleeping in my bed. She's beautiful and I'm happy she's back home. I drop my bags where I stand and climb in bed with her needing to kiss her. I wrap my arms around her and roll over on the bed, holding her on top of me. "I missed you. I love you, Ang." I kiss her and squeeze her in my arms.

She giggles, "I missed you, too." She rubs against me and my cock gets hard instantly. "Super D missed me, too."

"We both did."

She unhooks my belt and unbuttons my pants, "Can you get rid of these? They're in the way. I'm going to need this dress shirt you're wearing to go, too."

"Yes, ma'am."

She climbs off the bed and turns her back to me as she slides out of her pants and pulls her shirt off over her head, revealing her matching black lace panties and bra. "See anything you like?" She asks as she shakes her hips and ass at me.

I'm lying on top of the bed naked and she walks to me, "Everything, except the pretty lace needs to go."

"Do you want me naked?"

"Yes, and I've got something waiting for you," he says as he wraps his hand around his huge cock and gives it a stroke.

"I was hoping you'd be ready for me. I need you, D," she climbs on top of me straddling my waist. Her tone changes, sweeter, maybe more feminine, "I want all of you, it's more than sex. I love you, Doug. I need to be close to you. Please let me love you."

My already open heart about melts as her hands caress my chest and her words reach my ears. She strokes my hard cock with her hand and she shakes with need. She moves, guiding me in and takes me completely. Her whole body shivers and she sighs in relief. She lies down on me, her cheek to my chest and her hands on my shoulders. I hesitate, "Angie, should we talk about the birth control thing before we do this?"

"Your call. Always your call."

Fuck. "Ang?"

"Yeah?"

"You can trust me with everything, but you might not want to trust me with that decision."

She gazes up at me in contemplation, "Why not?"

I wrap my arms around her, "I'm going to come deep inside you every time. I can't help myself." I take a deep breath and whisper, "I want to knock you up. I want you barefoot in my kitchen with a baby belly full of Baby D."

"I'm okay with that," she says plainly.

I sit up with her in my arms and she wraps her legs around me. "I'm sorry, did you give me permission to get us pregnant?"

"Not exactly," she takes my hands and places them on her breasts. They're plump and round and obviously sensitive to my touch. "I haven't had my period since we were together. I'm late and I have symptoms. Your hands on me are driving me insane, I can hardly contain myself. Seriously D, I want to scream out your name."

"You're making me crazy. Are you pregnant with my baby?" She doesn't answer. "Angie? You need to answer me."

"It can't belong to anybody else, Mr. Fucked-me-bare-and-came-inside."

"Yeah, I did and it was better than I dreamt it'd be. I'm going to do it again." I grab her around the waist, holding her on my hard cock and she giggles.

Angie

I lean in to whisper in his ear, "I love you. I did a test this morning and it was positive. I'll schedule an appointment to get checked in a couple weeks. If not, keep doing what you do because I'm happy to give you what you want."

"I fucking love you," he takes my face in his hands and kisses me tenderly. He gazes into my eyes, "I promise to always take care of you and our Baby D's. Never leave me. Marry me and be my Mrs. D. Angie, seriously, please be my wife. There's nothing I want more in this world than to have you as my partner. Pregnant or not, Angie, I want you."

I laugh nervous, not often my defense mechanism kicks in, "I don't see a ring."

He reaches into the top drawer of his nightstand and pulls out a ring box, "I've had this ready to give you for almost three weeks. I had this whole elaborate plan to propose when you got here two weeks ago, but none of it matters." He opens the box and takes a simple diamond solitaire out of the box. He lifts me off of him, leaving me sitting naked on the bed and gets down on one knee at the bedside. He takes my hand in his and gazes up at me. His eyes teary and his whole body shaking, "Angie, I've loved you since the moment I met you and I want to spend my life with you. I know this is quick, but you've always been the one. We're a match. I promise to love you and take care of you for the rest of my life. There's no one else and there never will be. Please, make my dream come true and be my wife." He places the ring on my finger and holds my hand up to show me.

I lean down to kiss him and he takes me in his arms, naked on the floor. "Yes. Always, D. You and me, and whoever may come from us," I laugh happily. "Now, please love me all night, my Super D. Close this game."

ACKNOWLEDGMENTS

Thank you to my team for their continued work and support! Irene Johnson and Katrina Fair, my books would be ugly and editing nightmares without you.

Thank you to my Naughty Admins and readers for the daily inspiration you share with me, for sharing me with your friends, and for continuing to read my books.

Thank you to some of the best author friends a girl could have. Tonya Clark and Cassandra Robbins, you both rock socks in different ways.

PLAYLIST

"Angela" by The Lumineers
"Somebody" by Depeche Mode
"Dangerous Night" by Thirty Seconds to Mars
"Something Human" by Muse
"Simplify" by Young the Giant
"Walk on Water" by Thirty Seconds to Mars
"Heaven" by Bryan Adams
"Wonderwall" by Oasis
"Sex Type Thing" by Stone Temple Pilots

ABOUT THE AUTHOR

USA Today Bestselling Author Naomi Springthorp is a born and raised Southern California girl. She's a baseball freak who supports her team all season long and blatantly admires the athletes in those pants. Music has always been part of her life and she believes everything has a soundtrack. She loves her two feline fur babies, though they're not quite sure what to do with her.

She writes Baseball Romance, Romantic Comedies, 90s Throwback, and Contemporary Romance--all with heat and sometimes a little sweet.

Join her newsletter at
www.naomispringthorp.com/sign-up

facebook.com/naomithewriter

twitter.com/naomithewriter

instagram.com/naomispringthorp

amazon.com/author/naomispringthorp

bookbub.com/profile/naomi-springthorp

goodreads.com/naomithewriter

ALSO BY NAOMI SPRINGTHORP

An All About the Diamond Romance

The Sweet Spot

King of Diamonds

Diamonds in Paradise

Star-Crossed in the Outfield

The Closer

Falling for Prince

Up to Bat

Betting on Love

Just a California Girl

Jacks

Strings Attached

Standalone Novels & Novellas

Muffin Man

Finally in Focus

Confessions of an Online Junkie

Anthologies & Box Sets

Sacrifice for Love

Storybook Pub

Storybook Pub Christmas Wishes

Young Crush

Storybook Pub 2

Hate to Want You

Tricks, Treats, & Teasers

Caught Under the Mistletoe

All Access Pass